DEAD OF NIGHT

DEAD OF NIGHT

Dead For Good Book Three

STACY CLAFLIN

NOLON KING

STERLING & STONE

Chapter One

THE COLD AIR sent an icy chill down Brad Morris's spine despite his layers of warm clothes. The starless sky and the choppy harbor below made it feel more like the Arctic than the Pacific Northwest. And the light drizzle of rain didn't help matters.

"Are you sure about this?" Faye leaned over the edge, making the rowboat rock even more than it already was. "What if someone sees us?"

"Nobody will. That's why I chose this spot. No people or cameras."

"Have you dumped other bodies out here before?"

Brad drew in a deep breath as he continued rowing. His muscles burned and his three-ibuprofen headache still lingered. "Don't ask questions if you aren't sure you want the answers."

His wife sighed. "How much farther?"

"Just a little more." He rowed in silence for about five minutes before stopping. "This is a good spot. Nice and deep."

"Are you sure nobody will find him?"

"Yes." Brad pulled in the oars and looked over the plastic tarp, chains, and weights between the two of them. If his eyes hadn't adjusted, he wouldn't be able to see any of it. "You ready?"

Faye only made a noise.

"Is that a yes?"

"I can't believe we're doing this."

"We don't have another choice. Not if we want to keep our daughter from spending the rest of her life in jail."

"But it was self-defense. Surely any judge would understand that."

"Nate didn't have a weapon. I checked."

"He was threatening her with a video." Faye's voice wobbled. "He'd been antagonizing her, following her all night. Not to mention Nate's dad had threatened her before that."

"Hadley *killed* Nate. And she doesn't have a mark on her. This is the only thing we can do. Are you going to help me with this?"

"Yes."

The thick plastic crinkled as Brad inched his hands underneath the corpse. "Let's get this over with. We still have to get home and take care of everything there."

"I hope Hadley managed to fall asleep." Faye sighed before the plastic rumpled on her side.

Brad felt around the plastic and chains, until he was sure he had a good hold underneath the shoulders. "Ready to lift?"

"I can't believe we're doing this. Allison was my friend."

He understood Faye's distress — he wasn't a monster — but this wasn't the time to be sentimental. "It's done. We need to think about *our* family now. Lift on three."

"Okay."

The chain clanked on the wood as Faye struggled with her end.

Brad shouldn't have let her help. He was used to doing these jobs on his own.

Too late now.

"One. Two. Thr—"

"Wait."

He jolted to a stop. "What?"

"The boat won't tip over, will it?"

"No."

"You're sure?"

"Yes." He tried to keep the edge out of his voice. "I'm serious about needing to get this done. One—"

"How do we know nobody will find out we were out here?"

"Our phones are home, remember? If anyone needs to check the location, we were there all night. I didn't even go to the park to clean up Hadley's mess. Come *on*."

Faye sniffled.

"One. Two."

She gasped.

"Three." Brad hefted his end up. It was more than twice as heavy, thanks to the weights he'd placed under the plastic. They'd used several rolls of the most waterproof tape he had, and that added to the load.

Once the body was in the air, Brad inched toward the edge. "We'll swing and then throw. Again, on three. Ready?"

"Yes." Her voice squeaked.

Brad wanted to kick himself for bringing her. He should've had her stay home with Hadley. "One. Two. Three!"

The boat rocked as they swung Nate's body.

"Now." He let go.

It fell straight down, splashing them as the boat rocked violently.

He inched over to Faye and wrapped his arms around her. "I'm sorry I didn't insist you stay home."

She shook. "I'm just as involved with this as you are."

"You aren't used to this type of thing." He pulled out a flashlight and shined it on the water.

The body was already submerged, surfacing bubbles the only sign of its descent.

Faye snuggled closer. "No fish can get in there and chew off a finger or toe? Someone could find that and identify Nate."

"Nothing is getting inside that plastic."

"What if someone *does* find the body? Will there be any evidence linking to us? A stray fingerprint? Anything Hadley left behind? We can't possibly know about a stray hair. Or—"

Brad kissed her forehead. "No fingerprints, no hairs. But that doesn't matter since it won't be found."

"How do you know?"

"Because I'm that good. Have a seat. We need to get home and check on Hadley."

As he started rowing, Faye sniffled again.

He moved closer to the middle. "Come sit over here."

She snuggled against him, shaking as she choked back sobs. "How can you be so calm?"

"I've been doing this for years."

"Dumping bodies in the harbor?"

"Dealing with bodies."

"You always have to get rid of them?"

He rowed harder, eager to reach the shore. "No. I usually leave them to be discovered. But I've gotten rid of enough to know what I'm doing."

Faye shuddered. "I still can't believe you've been doing this for so many years."

"I'm making the world a safer place. Everyone is better off without the kind of people I'm assigned to kill."

"But Nate …"

"He shouldn't have been threatening Hadley."

"That didn't call for his murder!"

"It was an accident. You saw the look of horror in Hadley's eyes as she told us about it. What happened, happened. Now we have to protect our daughter. Right now that's all that matters."

"I can't believe she killed him."

Brad couldn't either, but didn't want to upset Faye further. "Accidents do happen."

"This is going to scar her for life! How is she going to live with this? She can't exactly talk to her therapist."

"I'll be her sounding board. My first kill stuck with me for a while. I know what it's like."

Faye sighed loudly.

"She'll get through this. I promise."

"This has been the worst year ever. And it isn't halfway through yet."

"It'll get better."

"You do realize we'll be grandparents by the time it's over, don't you? Hadley's still insisting on having that baby."

Brad rubbed her back. "Let's think about one thing at a time. Right now, we need to get home and make sure our daughter is okay. Then I have to double-check the park and make sure all the blood is gone."

"What about traces that you can't see?"

Pressure squeezed behind his eyes. "I have the technology to look. Like I said, I know what I'm doing. I've never been caught, and only suspected when framed."

"What are we going to do if people start questioning us?"

"I'll handle that."

"But someone could question me at work. Or Hadley, at school."

"You'll be ready when that time comes."

Thankfully, she let it go and silence settled between them. The only sound was the oars gliding through the water.

It gave him the time to finally *think*. There were so many new angles he needed to consider. Protecting his daughter and wife were number one. Hadley had killed a teenager, Faye was an accomplice in covering it up — and they had zero training.

He would need to teach them everything he knew about dealing with the cops. It was yet to be seen if they could handle the pressure. But none of them had any choice.

There couldn't be a single slip-up.

The oars made contact with the ground.

Now it was time to find out what they were all made of.

Chapter Two

THE HOUSE WAS quiet as Brad and Faye slid off their shoes and jackets. With any luck, all three kids would be sleeping. Brad couldn't wait to climb into bed and sleep on it before talking to Hadley. But he still needed to go back and give the park a thorough onceover.

His muscles throbbed with every step upstairs. As much as he wanted to send Faye to check on Hadley, it wouldn't be fair to either of them. Brad was the only one with the experience to deal with that conversation.

Good thing he was working from home. No way he could deal with going into BlueBlade after a night like this. Faye should take the day off. Hadley would definitely be staying home from school. That would give them the weekend to recover — and for Brad to prepare them for what came next.

After checking on Zeke and Luna, Faye took Brad by the hand. "They're sleeping. Are you ready to check on Hadley?"

"She's probably out, too."

7

"We can only hope. I don't know how she'd be able to sleep."

"Just like we will — because of pure exhaustion." Brad turned the knob and slowly opened the door. Faint light shone through the crack.

"She's still up?" Faye whispered.

"Probably went to sleep with her desk light on." He stepped inside the dim room, and a floorboard creaked under his weight.

Hadley bolted upright. "Dad?"

"Go back to sleep, hon." He fixed her covers.

"Did you … move it?"

"It's taken care of. Don't worry about it."

She clutched the blankets. "What did you do?"

"Put it somewhere nobody will ever find it."

"How can you be so sure?"

Brad stopped himself from saying he knew what he was doing.

Faye sat next to Hadley and wrapped her arms around her. "How are you doing?"

"I can't believe I killed Nate." Tears spilled onto her face.

Brad sat next to Faye. "Don't say that."

"But I did."

"We can't risk anyone else hearing."

"Who would? And it isn't like I'm going to say anything to anyone else. Are you sure I'm not going to jail?"

"Yes. You need to trust us."

"What's going to happen when the police start looking for him? His aunt probably already knows he's missing."

"She might think he's just breaking curfew. Teenagers sneak out all the time, right?" He stared at her stomach, the swelling proof of her many nights sneaking next door.

Hadley looked away.

Faye played with Hadley's hair. "We're going to take care of everything. The only thing we want you to worry about is taking care of yourself."

"What about school?"

"We'll have the teachers assign you work to do at home."

"Again?" Hadley glanced between the two of them. "Won't that look suspicious?"

"Not when you've been having health issues," Brad said.

"But people saw us talking after school. They'll know I'm guilty."

"Nobody knows anything," Brad said. "Let's go over the events from the time you saw Nate at school."

"Again?"

Faye pulled her closer. "We need to make sure we understand everything."

Hadley sighed dramatically and went over the same story she'd already told them, keeping every detail straight from the moment they ran into each other after school to him following her after she left and eventually to her accidental killing. Nothing had changed between any of the tellings, so she was giving them the truth.

"That isn't the story we'll tell anyone," Brad told Hadley. "You two had an awkward conversation but left on good terms. Then you went to the library and that restaurant, but you won't tell anyone about seeing him."

"What if they track his location on his phone or car?"

"Won't happen."

"How do you know?"

"I took care of them both."

Hadley gave him a double-take. "You moved his car?"

"Yes, and it's too old to have tracking. We're lucky Wes made him buy a clunker as a first car."

"But his phone—"

"Cell coverage is so spotty around the park, they'll be able to tell he was in the neighborhood, but they won't be able to pinpoint him there."

"What did you do with it?"

"You don't need to worry about the details. The less you know, the better."

"What about traffic cams?"

"They just prove you and Nate took similar routes."

"What if there's footage of him at the library or the restaurant?"

Faye rubbed her temples. "I never thought of any of this. What about *your* phone?"

"Burner from BlueBlade." Brad turned to Hadley. "Did you talk to him at either place?"

Hadley shook her head.

"If anyone notices, all they'll figure out is that he was following you." He stared at her. "You didn't interact with him after you left the school."

She nodded.

"Let me hear you say it."

"I didn't see him after talking to him at school."

Brad went over more details, making sure she knew exactly what to say when someone started asking questions. Once he was convinced she had the new story down, he kissed her forehead. "Lay down, kiddo. We all need our rest."

Hadley wrapped her arms around herself. "I don't know if I can ever sleep again."

"You will. Just remember that we'll make sure nothing happens to you."

She frowned, but did lie down.

Faye tucked her in, and after Hadley closed her eyes, Brad followed her to their room.

"I don't know if I'll ever be able to sleep again either," she said.

"You will." He rubbed her shoulders. "We all have plenty of experience speaking with the cops, thanks to me being framed for both Duke and Allison's murders."

Her eyes widened. "What if they try pinning this on you?"

"It won't hold up — just like the other two. I was nowhere near the kid. I think the last time our paths crossed was at Allison's funeral."

"What if they *do* suspect Hadley?"

He kissed her forehead. "There won't be any evidence. Speaking of that, I need to get to the park."

"What if someone sees you going there? That'll be suspicious."

Brad pulled his black hoodie up over his head. "Same as earlier — I'm taking the long route through the woods and avoiding all doorbell cams. It's going to take three times as long, but it's the only option."

"Maybe I should go with you."

"No — what I mean is, you get your rest."

"You need sleep, too."

"I can sleep in the morning. It's fine. This is more important."

She started to say something.

He brushed his lips across hers. "Climb into bed. I'll be back before you know it."

"You just said it'll take three times as long."

"And you won't miss me because you'll be in dream-land." He pulled the covers around her and went to the bathroom to prepare for round two.

Chapter Three

Zeke pushed the covers off and stared at the alarm blaring across the room. When that one went off, he had to get up right away. He rubbed his eyes and pushed unruly hair out of his face.

Something in the air felt out of sorts. Not that he believed in that woo-woo crap, but the feeling was definitely there. Maybe a bad dream lingering. That had to be it.

He forced his legs over the bed and pressed his feet on the cold hardwood.

The alarm kept screaming at him.

"I'm coming!" He turned it off and grabbed some clothes from the floor. They didn't smell bad and he hadn't worn his favorite gaming shirt all week, so nobody would bother him. He'd see if he could get Mom to do his laundry. It was his job, but more than half the time she'd do it if he pestered her enough.

Two steps into the hallway, he froze in place. Something was definitely off. The smells from Hadley's bathroom products should've overpowered him as soon as the door opened, and music should be coming from behind her closed door.

Instead, everything was dark and quiet. As he passed the bedrooms, all were closed except Luna's. Only the seven-year-old was awake?

Life was beginning to feel like a video game. And he'd just accepted the quest to figure out what on earth was going on.

He put his clothes on the odorless bathroom's counter, noting the lack of moisture on the mirrors. No dampness on the floor or in the shower.

His parents weren't letting Hadley stay home again, were they? She was getting all the luck these days. Maybe what Zeke needed was to get into real trouble. That seemed to be the way to his parents' attention.

He crept down the hall and pressed his ear against his older sister's door.

Silence.

If she wasn't getting ready, she wasn't going to school today.

She got all the breaks.

He looked in Luna's room. Dolls were spread everywhere, and both Mittens the cat and Grandma's dog Bingo were sleeping on the bed. Grandma was still in the hospital — otherwise Bingo would be in the guest room and she'd be downstairs making everyone breakfast.

Zeke went to his parents' door and listened. Dad was snoring. He'd been working from home lately, but was usually up to see everyone off. Why would he still be sleeping? Had he been up late? Maybe something had gone wrong.

His stomach dropped. Something hadn't happened with Grandma, had it?

He raced to the guest room and flung open the door.

Everything was as she'd left it before falling down the stairs and being rushed to the emergency room.

That didn't tell him anything.

Zeke went downstairs. Cartoons sounded, not that it surprised him. He already knew Luna was awake.

A drawer closed in the kitchen.

He hurried in to find Mom pouring cereal in a bowl.

"Luna! Come eat!" She shook her head at him. "Why aren't you dressed?"

"Why isn't Hadley going to school?"

"She had a long night."

"Puking?"

Luna skipped into the room, sat at her place, and dug into her food. "Who's puking?"

"Nobody." Mom glared at Zeke. "You know you aren't supposed to talk about her pregnancy to anyone outside of the family. Right?"

"Yes. You've made that abundantly clear. Doesn't make it right that she gets to stay home so much."

"That isn't your call. Why aren't you dressed? Your bus is going to be here soon."

"I have to take the bus?" His stomach twisted at the thought. Some of the wrestlers were on his route, and they always gave him a hard time.

"Yes. Hurry up."

He grumbled as he headed out of the kitchen.

"And make sure you eat some cereal! It's the most important meal of the day."

Normally, he'd be glad for the opportunity to pick a sugary cereal, but with everything else going on, it only irritated him. Just another way that everything was off.

He got ready and listened for activity in Hadley's room again. It was beyond unfair that she got away with so much. She'd snuck out of the house for who knew how long to sleep with Duke next door, and now she was pregnant with the dead twenty-five-year-old's baby. And their parents were letting her skip school because of it.

But if she didn't show up for her precious play's rehearsals, she'd get cut from the star role. At least *that* would be fair. Besides, did she really think she could actually pull that off? She would start showing her pregnancy at some point if she was serious about keeping the baby.

Between Hadley and Grandma, their family was so screwed up. No wonder they were all in counseling.

"Zeke!" Mom's voice came from downstairs.

He groaned, grabbed his backpack from his room, and trudged downstairs.

"You don't have time to eat before getting on the bus." She handed him a package of organic toaster pastries. Because being organic made them so much healthier. "Take these."

"Seriously? We're not allowed to eat on the bus."

"You should've thought about that before you took so long getting ready."

"You could drive me, you know."

"Honey, I can't. Not today. I'm sorry." She gave him a hug and nudged him toward the door. "Maybe tomorrow."

He glared at her. "This all sucks."

"You have no idea."

Zeke noticed how exhausted she looked. She'd covered dark circles under her eyes with makeup and her shirt was wrinkled. Her clothes were never less than perfect — it was obvious where Hadley got that habit from.

"You okay?" he asked.

She drew in a deep breath and looked lost in thought for a moment before nodding. "Everything will be fine. Hurry up. I think I hear your bus."

He wanted to press for more information, but that

would have to wait. The truth would come out eventually, even if he had to dig a while to find it.

Mom gave him a hug before pushing him out the door.

Zeke shoved earbuds in before getting on the bus. No music played, but at least he could pretend not to hear the wrestlers making fun of him.

Luckily, Wynn was also taking the bus today.

Zeke plopped down next to him and pulled out the earbuds.

"Rough morning?" Wynn dog-eared his sci-fi novel and shoved it in his bag.

"My family sucks."

"Join the club."

Zeke slumped lower in the seat, as if that would keep him from hearing the insults aimed at them. "What'd yours do?"

Wynn sighed dramatically. "You know how I told you about my dad's new girlfriend?"

"The one with the big mole on her chin?"

"No. That was the last one. This one has the big ears and tries to be cool. She started playing HardCorps. Sent me a friend request and everything. Dad says I have to accept."

"Lame."

"Exactly. So, why does your family suck this week?"

"Nothing new. Hadley gets away with murder. I swear, if she really did kill someone, she'd never get in trouble for it."

"At least you don't have to deal with stepsisters." Wynn rolled his eyes. "Mine are straight out of a nightmare."

"I thought your mom was going to divorce that guy."

"No. Now they're in love again."

"How are we expected to put up with all of this stuff?"

Wynn shrugged. "Got me. What did Hadley do this time?"

"Nobody will tell me, but she gets to skip again."

"We need to get her to tell us her secrets."

"I wish." Zeke glanced up at the rearview mirror to make sure the driver wasn't watching, then opened the toaster pastry. The foil yelled almost louder than all the kids around him.

"No breakfast?" Wynn lifted a brow.

"Nothing." He slouched lower and scarfed it down as fast as he could.

Hopefully he'd know what was going on with his family by the time he got home.

Chapter Four

Brad turned down the police scanner so Hadley wouldn't hear it if she woke. If he hadn't been plagued with dreams about Nate's death, he'd still be asleep too, instead of locked in his office. But even though he'd taken so many precautions scrubbing the blood and dumping the body, there was still the chance of numerous things going wrong. He normally put more time and effort into the planning stage than the actual killing.

But this was a whole different beast. His baby girl had done the deed. Accidentally.

He could *not* let her get caught. That family had been threatening her. Trying to pin a murder on Brad.

It was no wonder she'd lashed out. He couldn't say he'd have done anything differently if he'd been in her shoes.

Now he would put all of his training and experience to good use, for her sake.

So far, there was no mention of Nate's disappearance. He refreshed his social media feed. Still nothing. Checked several of the major news sites. Nothing, but that wasn't surprising. They would hardly cover a teen staying out all night. That had to be a common occurrence.

He leaned closer to the scanner. Just a home invasion and a collision on the freeway.

Brad rested his eyes and tried to ignore the exhaustion squeezing every inch of his body. Maybe he should give in and try to get some more sleep. He'd only had a few hours, and he'd need to be on top of his game if anyone came asking questions.

But first, he needed to check on Hadley.

She was sound asleep.

Relief washed through him, and he trudged back to his bed. Checked social media one more time. Then fell asleep the moment his head hit the pillow.

When he woke, bright light shone through the blinds. He felt far more rested than before.

Just past noon. A few more hours of sleep had been just what he needed.

He got up and checked on Hadley again.

She was in bed, scrolling on her phone.

"How'd you sleep?"

"Horrible. I kept waking up."

Brad rubbed her shoulders. "I had a lot of frustrating dreams myself."

Hadley stared at him, her eyes huge with fear. She looked more like the little girl she used to be than the seventeen-year-old she was. "I don't want to go to jail, Daddy."

His heart shattered. "You won't. I'll make sure of that."

"How?"

"Nobody's going to find the body. And without that, they can't possibly link you to his death."

"I was the last one to see him alive."

"There's no way to prove that."

"What about all the blood?" She squeezed a blanket, making her knuckles whiten.

"It's gone from the park. I'm going to burn our clothes and the knife to ash."

"How? Don't you need special equipment to get it hot enough?"

He patted the top of her head as he rose. "You're too smart for your own good."

"Well?"

Brad pictured the incinerator in a secret room at work behind Kurt's office. "I have access to the necessary equipment."

Hadley didn't look like she believed him.

"I don't want you worrying about anything."

"What if something goes wrong? Will you tell me?"

"Of course."

She narrowed her eyes.

"I *will*."

"Okay."

"You're feeling okay? No bleeding?"

Hadley shook her head. Then she looked away quickly.

"What's the matter?"

"Nothing. I'm fine."

Brad snorted. "When a woman says she's fine, the opposite is often true. What's going on?"

She played with a strand of hair. Didn't look at him.

"Hadley."

"Okay, okay." She finally turned to him, tears welling. "Nate's blood got in my mouth and eyes. What if I got a disease?"

She hadn't mentioned that before. "Did he *have* a disease?"

"I don't know."

"Did he have a reputation for sleeping around?"

"The opposite, actually."

"Was that true?"

Hadley shrugged.

Brad drew a deep breath. "The fact that he wasn't known for getting around is a good sign."

"But how will I know? I don't want to have that in the back of my mind all the time."

"We'll get you tested. When's your next appointment?"

"I don't know, but I don't want to wait that long. I want to go today."

Brad paced.

What else could possibly go wrong?

"Dad?"

"Let me look into it."

"Look into it? Can't you just take me to that blood draw place at the hospital?"

"You still need a doctor's order. People can't just walk up and get any blood work they want."

"Why not?"

He drew a deep breath. "Doctors have to read the report. Like I said, I'll see what I can do. I need to think of a reason to give for wanting the test — something other than the fact that a dead kid's blood got in your mouth."

"Don't say that so loud!"

"Nobody else is home."

"Just say I'm concerned. I'm a pregnant teenager, so they probably won't even question it."

"Do you want to make the appointment?"

Hadley's face paled. "No."

"You want to raise a baby, but you can't make an appointment?"

She folded her arms. "I haven't *decided* if I want to raise it or not. All I know is I don't want to get rid of it. The baby is all I have left of—"

His phone rang: *Kurt.*

"I have to take this." Brad walked toward the door. "I suggest you call your own doctor in the meantime."

Hadley said something, but he was already in the hallway. He closed the door between them and accepted the call.

"Brad here."

No response. But the call had already gone to voicemail.

Brad marched to his office to think.

Now they had to worry about Hadley having gotten a disease from Nate. What if she accidentally let it slip why she was worried? She was under so much stress, it could happen.

And he'd told her to call her doctor.

He raced back to her room. "Did you call yet?"

"You haven't given me any time."

"Just let me or Mom handle it. You should focus on resting."

"Why'd you change your mind?"

"Because you need take it easy. You have enough to deal with as it is."

"Okay."

"Just don't tell anyone anything about any of this."

She looked at him like he was crazy. "Why would I do that? I could go to jail!"

"Exactly. You can't let it slip out. Remember our story?"

"Yes."

"Good. Stick with that. Don't bring up Nate with anyone, ever."

"Trust me, I won't." Her voice cracked. "I don't even want to think about him."

Brad's phone buzzed with a text.

Kurt telling him to call back immediately.

Of all the days.

He wrapped his arms around Hadley. "This will all work out. Nobody's going to find Nate, or any evidence of what happened. I triple-checked everything."

His phone buzzed again.

"Do you need to answer that?"

"Kurt can wait. I need to know you understand what I'm telling you."

"You don't think anyone will find out about Nate."

"It's a fact — not just something I think."

She sighed.

"Do you trust me?"

"How do you *know*?"

He couldn't blame her for doubting. She didn't know that he was an assassin, rather than a knife salesman. "I have some experience in the matter."

She lifted a brow. "You do?"

His phone buzzed again.

He tossed it toward her door. "Yes."

"How?"

His phone rang.

Brad resisted the urge to stomp on it. That would only add to his problems.

"What kind of experience?" Hadley asked.

His mind raced for a simple answer. "You know I give knife safety trainings, right?"

"Yeah, but what does that have to do with anything?"

His phone rang again.

"Maybe you should get that."

He tugged on his hair. "Kurt can wait. You're more important. What was I saying?"

"Knife safety trainings have something to do with hiding bodies."

"No, not hiding bodies. Blood. It all comes down to the blood. I know how to clean it from things so it leaves no trace." That was the simple answer. He didn't feel like explaining luminol and black lights.

"So, you used bleach at the park?"

He shook his head. "That isn't as thorough as everyone thinks. Can you just trust that I have this handled? I know what I'm doing, but I don't have the time to explain everything."

His phone rang again as if to prove his point. "I'm going to get that. Do you trust me?"

"I guess."

He gritted his teeth. "That doesn't sound very convincing."

"I never thought of you like that."

"Start thinking of me as a blood expert."

"And what about the body?"

The phone rang again.

Now he was really tempted to break it. "Nobody will *ever* find it."

"How can you be so sure?"

"Because I am. I can go over the details with you later, if that'd make you feel better. But for now, I better get back to Kurt before he has a conniption fit or fires me. Okay?"

Hadley nodded. "I'm going to lie down. I'm getting a headache."

"You and me both."

His phone rang again.

Chapter Five

BRAD LOCKED his office door and stared at his phone's screen. He'd missed Kurt's last call, but that meant it would only be a few moments before he called again.

What had him so eager to talk to Brad now? It was a game of cat-and-mouse with him. Kurt was either his best friend or he avoided Brad like the plague.

There was no reason for his boss to want to buddy up, so why was he so desperate to talk?

His heart dropped to the floor.

Could he know about Nate?

No. That was impossible.

Or was it? Did he somehow know what Brad had been up to? He couldn't. Brad had left his phone — a company phone — at home while he'd been out all night taking care of everything.

There was no way Kurt knew what Hadley had done. And even if he did, why would he care? It wouldn't get back to BlueBlade.

Brad's ringing phone jolted him from his thoughts.

He accepted the call. "Brad here."

"Where have you been?"

"Taking care of my sick child." That was mostly true.

"How sick?"

"She'll be fine. What do you need?"

"I need you back in the store."

Brad swore. "*That's* why you've been calling nonstop? I thought someone was dead."

"And it took you that long to answer?"

"I was taking care of a sick child. Why do you need me in so badly?"

"We're short-staffed."

"You know what I'm dealing with here. That's why I'm 'working on the website' at home. All I can focus on right now is my targets — which is the only thing that matters, really."

Kurt muttered something. "You can't come in? With Rose in jail and you out, that's all we can handle. And now Scott's injured."

Scott was one of the few guys that had been there longer than him. He'd given Brad advice when he was a rookie.

"Was he targeted on a hit too?" Brad exclaimed. "Is he okay?"

"Car accident — totally unrelated. But he's going to be out of commission for a while. Cracked ribs and a concussion."

Brad winced. "Sorry to hear about that, but there's no way I can get away. Like I said, I've got a kid home sick and I have to pick up my mother from the hospital. Can't leave either of them home unsupervised."

"Isn't Faye opening a salon at home?"

"Not yet. There's a lot to do to get the house ready for her to work here."

"That's the only thing in your way?"

"Yeah."

Rustling noises sounded on the other end of the line. "I have a guy. He'll be in touch."

"A guy?"

"My contractor. He and his team will get the salon set up before you know it."

Brad hated to get Faye's hopes up before he knew they could afford it. "We can talk to him about an estimate—"

"I guarantee it'll be extremely affordable. Gary owes me a big favor."

"But it's still a big financial commitment. I can't be sure—"

"If it's more than you can swing right now, I've got it covered. I need you on the job."

Brad stared at his screen in disbelief. Shook his head to clear it. Kurt was willing to help pay for a new addition to his house to avoid giving Brad a little more time off?

Who needed killing that urgently?

Or was this a way for Kurt to get his claws into Brad's family?

Once Brad owed him — and Faye would owe him too — he might not be able to say no to Kurt until the debt was paid.

He couldn't afford that. He'd raid his retirement account and his children's college funds before he'd be Kurt's puppet.

"I'll pay you back, of course."

"We can talk about the details once you're back. Should I have Gary call you or Faye?"

Brad blinked a few times. "Faye's the one with the plans drawn."

"Tell her Gary will be in touch within the hour. Make sure she answers when he calls. Got it?"

"Yes. And I'm serious, I—"

Kurt hung up before Brad could finish the sentence.

Brad stared at his screen in disbelief. Shook his head to clear it.

What was going on?

But there was no way to figure that out without going in. And he needed to speak with Faye. Not just about the contractor, but about Hadley's appointment.

Everything was spiraling.

He drew a deep breath and walked to the window.

Cora from next door was outside with her two little kids and the baby in a wrap around her. A lady in a pencil skirt who had a streak of blue in her black hair was going door to door, probably either selling something or trying to save souls. Lucas turned the corner with his little dog, who was dressed a pink rain jacket.

What he wouldn't give for a simple life with normal worries.

He called Faye, not expecting her to answer. She was usually with a client.

"Hi, honey. How's it going?"

She must've been between styling appointments.

He explained Hadley's situation first, careful not to use Nate's name.

Faye gasped in horror. "Do you think she actually has something?"

"I hope not. She said he had a reputation for being a prude."

"Let's hope that's right."

"Can you call her doctor and find out if she can get the tests? I told her to, but I don't think she will. I can take her when I go to pick up Mom from the hospital later."

"Yeah, I'll call. I'm on lunch, so it's perfect timing."

"One more thing," he said quickly before she could end the call.

"What's that?"

"Keep your ringer on, and answer right away when you get a call in less than an hour."

"Huh?" Faye said.

"Kurt wants me back in the office, so he's paying his contractor to build your salon. But you have to answer when he calls. His name is Gary."

"Are you serious?" Faye exclaimed.

"They're short-staffed, and building your salon is probably pocket change for Kurt."

"This can't be happening."

"It is."

Faye gasped. "Someone's calling right now."

"Answer it. And don't forget to call about Hadley."

"I won't! Love you."

"You too." He ended the call and rubbed his temples.

Just what he needed on top of everything else — noise from construction all day for who knew how long. His mother would probably hate it, too. But he couldn't bring her upstairs. She'd be right across the hall from the noise.

They might have to spend the days at her house. At least it would be quiet. Plus, it would give her the chance to be in her own home for a while each day.

And Brad would be able to spend more time going through his dad's office. He'd already found proof that his father had worked at the Slippery Fish car wash. The old man had been an assassin, too.

Brad had barely had time to process the news before Hadley came home a bloody, blubbering mess, having accidentally killed Nate.

Yes, spending the days at his mom's house was the ideal situation. And the construction gave him the perfect excuse.

Feeling relieved, he sat at his desk and checked online

for any mention of Nate. No news sites mentioned the boy's disappearance, and he couldn't find a single mention on social media.

So far, so good. But that would only last so long. Nate's aunt was bound to start looking for him soon, if she wasn't already. Maybe she believed the myth about having to wait twenty-four hours before declaring someone missing.

That would work in their favor.

He turned on the police scanner. Barely had five seconds to listen before his phone rang.

Faye.

He accepted the call. "Did you speak with Gary?"

"He's going to start tomorrow!"

"That soon?"

"Yeah. Can you believe it?"

"No. Seriously, tomorrow?"

She squealed. "He's coming by the salon later to talk about the plans. And starting tomorrow. Isn't that crazy?"

"I'd say so."

"You have to thank Kurt for me. I don't know how he pulled those strings, but I never imagined this could happen so quickly."

Brad rubbed his temples. With so many people coming into the house for the construction and then later for the salon, he needed to heighten his office security. A single coded lock wouldn't do anymore. He would need an alarm and a backup lock. Or perhaps move some of his job-related items to his mom's house.

"Are you listening?" Faye asked.

"What was the part you just said?"

"I spoke with Hadley's doctor, and she said she'd put in the order for the blood work at the hospital. She can show up any time for the blood draw."

"Perfect."

Faye talked excitedly about the salon for a minute before saying goodbye.

Brad closed his eyes for a moment. His lids were heavy enough to fall asleep.

Maybe a nap wasn't such a bad idea. He would need the rest before getting through the remainder of his day.

He checked on Hadley, who was on her phone.

"Shouldn't you be doing homework?"

"Are you kidding? I have to see if anyone from school is talking about Nate being missing."

"Are they?"

"No."

"I'm going to take a quick nap. Why don't you get a shower? We're going to the hospital to pick up Grandma and get your blood drawn."

She arched a brow. "Do I need another shower? I took five last night."

"Take one or don't. Just be ready to leave soon."

"Okay." She ran hands through her hair. "It's so clean, it's squeaky."

"I'm sure you're fine." He went to his room and climbed under the covers, setting his alarm, and falling asleep as soon as he closed his eyes.

The beeping sounded. Time to get up already?

He tried to wake up, not feeling any more rested than before.

Not that it mattered. It was time for the hospital.

Chapter Six

Zeke placed his tray next to Wynn's and sat.

"Did you figure out what's going on with your family?" Wynn slurped his chocolate milk.

"You know, that's why we'll never sit at the popular table."

"That isn't the only reason." Wynn pointed to Zeke's *Short Circuit* T-shirt. "And besides, I don't want to sit at that table."

"Neither do I."

Laughter sounded from where the popular kids always ate. Ben from the chess club walked away from that table with spaghetti sauce smeared on his face, muttering to himself.

"I don't even want to sit *near* them." Wynn slurped his milk again, moving the straw around. "It isn't safe."

"You aren't going to get any more milk out of there, you know."

"I can get a few more drops. You really haven't thought of anything? Hadley must've done something. Is she boinking a teacher now?"

Heat crept into his face. He hated that everyone knew about his sister and Duke. "Shut up. That's my sister you're talking about."

"You can't stand her."

"So? Doesn't mean you can talk about her like that. You're my best friend."

"Okay, whatever. Who — I mean what — do you think she did this time?" Wynn snickered.

Zeke glared at him. "I don't know. I'm going to have to play detective at home tonight. But with the way everyone was acting, it has to be big."

"You sure you can't think of anything? I'm really getting curious. Is it that new neighbor? He's not much older than Duke was."

Zeke balled up and threw his napkin at him.

Wynn burst out laughing and tossed it back.

Elena Campbell came to their table and stopped. She looked right at Zeke. "Have you seen my brother?"

"Joey or Nate?"

"Nate. You and your sister are friends with him, right?"

Zeke shrugged. "I wouldn't really go that far."

"You guys hang out."

"Once. He's nice. That doesn't make us friends. Just neighbors, I guess. Why?"

She frowned and sighed. "He didn't come home last night, which isn't like him. And his phone keeps going straight to voicemail. My aunt is freaking out. I told her I'd ask around."

"Maybe he went to a friend's house," Wynn offered.

"Without telling anyone?"

"He's a senior, right?"

"Yeah. But he always calls when he's late." She turned back to Zeke. "Does your sister know where he is?"

"How would I know?"

"She's your sister."

Zeke crossed his arms. "Doesn't mean we talk."

"Look. If you hear anything about Nate, let us know."

"I don't have your number."

Elena rattled off the digits.

"Hold *on*." Zeke pulled out his phone and made sure none of the cafeteria workers were looking his way before going into his contacts list. "Now."

She said them again. "Got it?"

He read them off.

"If you hear *anything*. Seriously, my aunt is really worried."

Wynn leaned forward. "What about you?"

"Like you said, he's a senior. And he was pretty upset about Dad getting arrested. But still, it really isn't like him. He's the responsible one." Elena headed to another table.

Wynn stared at Zeke.

"What?"

"Hadley *is* friends with him."

"How would I know?" He dug into his spaghetti.

"You told me about the movie and ice cream."

Zeke swallowed. "My parents made us go to the movies, and Nate was just there. We sat with him because, why not? Then he suggested the ice cream place because they were having some kind of sale. It really wasn't a big deal. Not like we hung out after that."

"Do you think he ran away?"

"How would I know?"

"Was he acting weird?"

"I don't *know*." Zeke took a big bite of warm peaches, hoping Wynn would take the clue.

"Has Hadley been acting strange?"

He chewed and swallowed. "Always."

"Do you think they had something going on?"

"I wouldn't know."

"I said, do you *think*?"

Zeke shrugged. "What's the big deal?"

"All morning you've been upset because your family is acting like they're hiding something. Do you think it has anything to do with Nate?"

"I don't see why it would."

"Your parents are friends with his parents."

"Our moms were. Not our dads. Not even close."

Wynn's eyes widened with curiosity. "They didn't like each other?"

"I told you about that."

"Yeah, I guess I remember something about that. Do you think there's a connection?"

"I think you *want* there to be one. I'm pretty sure he and Hadley don't hang out."

"Pretty sure?"

"It's not like I pay attention to what my sister does. Little Miss Perfect just wants everyone to focus on her. I refuse."

They finished their meal in silence before heading to their lockers. Zeke's neck and head ached.

"You ready for that math quiz?" Wynn asked.

Zeke groaned. "I just want to go home and play Hard-Corps. Don't want to think about anything else."

"That'd be the life, only having to worry about that."

"Yeah." He shoved his books into his bag. "See you in math."

"See ya." Wynn waved before they parted ways.

Zeke went to the water fountain, hoping that might help with his headache. What he really needed was a normal life and a normal family.

Was that so much to ask?

He headed toward his history class.

Halfway there, a lady stopped him. He didn't recognize her, and he was pretty sure the school didn't allow teachers to have blue streaks in their hair. This woman had a prominent one that stood out from her black hair.

"You're Zeke, right?"

He eyed her with suspicion. "Yeah. Who are you?"

"My name is Jacinta Parks, and I'm looking into the disappearance of Nate Campbell."

"Now it's a disappearance?"

"You know about that?" Her eyes widened slightly.

"His sister was just telling me he didn't come home last night."

"You're friends with him, aren't you?"

Zeke's headache worsened. "He's my neighbor."

"But you wouldn't call yourself his friend?"

"No. We didn't hang out like that."

"What about your sister?"

Zeke took a step back. "What's with all the questions?"

"There's a missing person."

"I don't see how I can help with that. I don't know where he is and I have no idea where he would go."

"Are you sure about that?"

"Of course I am. I need to get to class."

"People keep saying you and your sister are his friends."

"Well, people don't know what they're talking about."

The woman pursed her lips. "Where's your sister?"

"She goes to the high school."

"I'm aware of that, but she doesn't appear to be there today, either."

The warning bell rang.

"Call her if you're so worried about it. I have to get to class." Zeke started to walk away.

"Let the family know if you hear from him!"

He ignored her and hurried away. Who was that woman? Nate's aunt? She'd said for him to call 'the family' if he found out where Nate was. That made it sound like she wasn't one of them.

But he had enough other things to worry about besides Nate. Something was going on with *his* family. Both Dad and Hadley were staying home for the day, and Mom gave him toaster pastries for breakfast.

Maybe it was a full moon, and everyone was acting weird. Even Wynn was trying to be a detective. Yeah, it had to be the moon making everyone act up.

Or what if there actually was a connection between Nate's family and his? But that seemed unlikely. It wasn't like any of them were friends with the Campbells anymore. Allison was dead and Hadley had stopped hanging out with Nate, at least as far as Zeke knew. It wasn't like he kept up with her.

Nothing added up, unless someone had made friends with the aunt. Unlikely, given that Wes had just been arrested.

Zeke raced into his classroom just as the final bell rang.

The teacher gave him an annoyed look before telling them to open their textbooks.

He hurried to his seat and piled his things on the desk, but his mind was racing, trying to find a connection between anyone in his family and any of the Campbells.

The teacher started asking questions. Zeke would have to wait to think about this until after school.

He hoped he wouldn't be able to find any connections at all.

Chapter Seven

BRAD LOOKED around the makeshift bedroom. It was pretty good for what it was — converted from the side room just off the entry with some portable privacy walls.

"I really don't mind it." Mom smiled. "I appreciate all the work you put into this."

"We would all prefer you to be upstairs in an actual room, but this is the doctor's orders."

She cringed.

"Are you okay?" He rushed to her side, ready to help with whatever she needed.

"Just remembering the fall."

He tried not to shudder at the memory of hearing her tumble down the stairs and finding her at the bottom. Mere minutes after finding out about Hadley's pregnancy.

Worst year ever. It was enough to make him want to fast forward through the rest of it.

Brad put his hand on Mom's shoulder. "I don't want to think about it, either. But hopefully soon, you'll be able to move back into the guest room."

"Or my own house."

He frowned.

"You don't think I'll ever live there again?"

"That isn't what I said."

"You didn't have to."

"Mom, all any of us want is for you to be safe. And we're more than happy to have you here."

She sighed.

"I know it's hard. None of us wanted any of this for you. It isn't fair."

"Can I at least help with dinner? Or am I too fragile for that?"

He looked at her arm cast, her foot cast, and the stitches on her face. He couldn't even see how her ribs were covered to protect the fractures. "It's not about you being fragile. Your body needs to heal. Let us take care of you for a while."

Brad helped her to the living room where Luna was playing Candy Land with one of her dolls. "Can Grandma join you?"

"Yeah!" Luna cleared the board and turned to Brad's mom. "What color do you want?"

"You pick, sweetheart."

Brad helped his mom onto the couch and left the room. He rubbed his temples, trying to put off the headache that had harangued him since the hospital. Maybe before. Everything was blurring together. It was getting to the point that he could hardly differentiate one day from the next, much less hour to hour.

He checked his phone for any mention of Nate on the news. It was only a matter of time before the missing kid was a piping-hot topic.

Two of the local stations had stories about Nate on the front pages of their websites.

Hadley came downstairs, her hair pulled back and her

face looking fresh. She rubbed her arm.

Brad turned off his phone's screen and turned to her. "How are you feeling?"

"Like I've been stabbed with a needle." Her mouth gaped. "I shouldn't have said stabbed."

He stepped closer to her. "You didn't *stab* him."

"No, but I—"

"Put it out of your mind. It was self-defense. You or him, and now you're alive. That's all that matters."

"But he wasn't trying to kill me."

"Doesn't matter. Was still self-defense. Are you hungry? There's still some of that soup from earlier."

"Won't Mom get mad if I ruin my dinner?"

"She's not going to get mad at you for anything. If you're hungry, eat."

Hadley hesitated. "Okay."

"Do you want me to warm it up?"

"Pretty sure I can handle it."

"If you *do* need help, let me know."

"I'll be fine." She plodded into the kitchen.

He was tempted to follow her and grab a beer. More than anything, he needed to unwind. But Faye wasn't home from the salon yet, and Brad had to manage everyone else until she got there. And even when she did arrive, he couldn't expect that she would suddenly take over and he could simply chill.

Everyone needed him.

Maybe he should make dinner. But one quick look through the fridge and pantry told him that he didn't know what he was doing. He could dump soup into a pot, but not much else.

That wasn't true. He could grill meat like it was nobody's business. Then Faye wouldn't have to worry about cooking. She was bound to be exhausted after last night.

Brad went outside to check how much propane he had, but stopped short. It was pouring rain. Gushing out over the gutters like a waterfall where the leaves always got stuck.

Great. One more thing to take care of. And there was no way he could grill anything in this weather. He really needed to build a covering over their patio.

He headed back inside, deflated.

"Daddy!" Luna called.

"Yes, sweetie?" He shook the rain off before heading over to the kitchen.

"Can we get Chinese? Both Grandma and I are in the mood. Please?" She batted her lashes.

He turned to his mom. "Is that what you really want?"

"Sounds heavenly compared to the hospital food."

"I'll order takeout." And at least nobody would have to cook anything.

"Yay!" Luna pumped her fist in the air.

Just after he placed the order, a key jingled in the front door.

Faye stepped inside, beaming. She threw her arms around him, squeezing tightly, and kissed him passionately.

"Maybe I should order takeout more often."

"What? No. That's for setting up the contractor. Gary said my plans are totally doable. He's actually starting tomorrow! Can you believe it?"

"Wow, that's fast."

She grinned. "I know. We need to start clearing out that room."

The room they'd been using for storage.

He checked the time. "I'll pick up the food, then we can get started after we eat."

"I'm going to start now." She hung up her coat and kicked off her shoes. "Unless someone needs me. How's Hadley? Your mom?"

"Hadley's eating some soup and Mom's playing Candy Land with Luna."

"Great. I'll get Zeke to help me."

Ding-dong!

They exchanged confused glances.

"Are you expecting anyone?" he asked.

She shook her head before answering the door.

It was the lady with the blue streak in her hair who had been going door-to-door earlier.

Brad stood behind Faye. "We're not interested in buying anything."

"I'm not selling anything." The woman held out her hand. "I'm Jacinta Parks. Are you Brad and Faye Morris?"

He stepped next to Faye. "We are. What can we help you with, Jacinta?"

"May I come in?"

"We're quite busy at the moment, and we have a full house—"

"It'll only take a minute, and it's pouring out here."

He drew a deep breath as Faye invited her in. Had she forgotten everything he'd told her?

Jacinta eyed the temporary walls for his mom's makeshift room.

Brad offered no explanation. "What is it you need? We have things we need to do. People to take care of."

"I understand. This won't take long. I'm a social worker for—"

"You're from the hospital?" Brad interrupted. "I didn't expect you so soon."

"The hospital?" Her brows lifted in confusion. "No. I'm here on behalf of Nate Campbell."

His heart skipped a beat, but he barred the surprise from his face. "Nate? Why does he need a social worker? I thought his aunt was adopting him."

"This has nothing to do with the adoption."

"Oh?" Faye looked genuinely surprised. "Is everything okay?"

Jacinta looked at them both before replying. "Nate didn't come home after school yesterday. He's been missing for a full day now."

"Oh, no. That's awful." Faye covered her mouth. "Does anyone have any idea what happened to him?"

Brad was impressed with her acting. Especially given how she had mishandled things after Duke's death.

"Nobody knows anything," Jacinta said. "It would appear that he just vanished after leaving the school yesterday."

"That's scary," Brad replied. "I'm sure the family is out of their minds with worry. I know I would be if that was one of my kids."

She nodded, her expression somber.

Faye stepped closer. "Is there anything we can do?"

"Actually, yes. I would love to speak with Hadley and Zeke."

Faye stiffened.

Brad put his arm around her. "Why do you need to talk with our children?"

"As I've been speaking with neighbors and Nate's friends, both of their names keep coming up."

"I'm not sure why that is." Brad studied the social worker, trying to read any micro expressions that would tell him what she wasn't saying out loud. "Our kids are friendly with him, but not close."

Jacinta's eyes widened slightly, and only for a moment. "What makes you say that?"

"Because it's true," Faye said quickly. "They really only know each other because Allison — Nate's mom — and I were friends before she died. They had no interactions before that."

"I see. But didn't they spend time together after her death?"

Brad's pulse drummed in his ears. Game time. "They ran into each other from time to time, which is understandable. The Campbells live around the corner, and Hadley and Nate both go to the same school."

The social worker nodded. "Would you mind me speaking with them? It'll only take a moment."

"Actually, this isn't a good time."

Her brows lifted. "Why? What's been—"

"My mother has been having health issues. She's staying with us, and the kids are very close to her."

"Like I said, it won't take long. And they might know something that could help us find a missing child."

"Child?" Brad countered.

Jacinta's expression soured. "He's in high school and under his aunt's care. Why are you reluctant to help us find him?"

"I'm more than happy to help — just not at the expense of my children. They've been through a lot lately. Give me your card, and I'll ask them about Nate when I can. If they tell me anything that could help, I promise to call you immediately." He held out his hand for a card.

"I don't have one at the moment." Jacinta shook her head. "It'll only take a few minutes, then I'll be out of your hair."

"You're a social worker, but you don't have a card?"

"Not on me."

"That seems odd. Where's your office? What department do you work for?"

Faye nudged him. "Brad. Don't be rude."

He looked at Faye as if she were crazy. The woman was trying to interrogate their children, and one of them was guilty! He returned his attention to Jacinta — if that was her real name. "We'll do whatever we can to help — hand out fliers, set up a vigil, join a search team — but we draw the line at our kids. I've already explained myself. Do we need to get an attorney?"

"I could return with a warrant, but I'm sure you don't want it to come down to that."

Brad exchanged a confused look with Faye. He didn't have a law degree, but he was pretty sure only police dealt with warrants.

There was definitely something off about this woman.

He pulled out his phone. "Actually, a call to my attorney is sounding better by the moment."

Jacinta took a step closer. "You do realize that makes you look guilty."

"Of what? Protecting my children?"

"Weren't you a suspect in Allison's murder?"

"*Neighbors* pointed fingers. You'll notice who was arrested for that crime."

She didn't respond.

"Her husband. He killed her."

"What's your point?" Jacinta stiffened.

"People keep blaming this family for things that go wrong in this neighborhood, but you know what? It ends up being someone else, *every time*. So, if you'll excuse us, we need to take care of our family now."

"Do you have something to hide?"

He stared her down. "Absolutely nothing."

She stood taller. "I'm going to be back, Mr. Morris. I highly recommend you consider allowing your children to speak with me."

"If you want to speak with any of us, you'll need to go through my attorney."

"Is that a threat?"

"Does it need to be?"

Jacinta glowered at Brad before leaving, slamming the door behind her.

Faye leaned against the wall and pressed her palm to her chest. "I can't believe that just happened."

"Why'd you tell me not to be rude to her?"

"I was playing the part."

He paced. "I don't think she's really a social worker."

"Why not? Because of the blue in her hair?"

"She didn't have a card."

"So? Maybe she ran out. She did say she'd been talking to a lot of people."

He checked the time. "I need to get the food. I'm going to see if I can reach an attorney."

"If you don't think Jacinta is a social worker, why bother?"

"Because I need to be prepared. Whatever her real role, I can tell she isn't going to give up." He gave her a kiss. "You did great. For now, focus on emptying that room. Get Zeke to help, like you said. I'll be back with dinner soon."

"You don't think anyone will figure out what really happened?"

"No reason anyone should. And more importantly, there's no evidence. It's all been washed away."

She shuddered.

He pulled her close. "I know what I'm doing. Trust me."

"I do."

"Then put all your attention on the new salon. I'll deal

with Jacinta Parks, Detective Stewart, and anyone else who comes our way."

Faye nodded.

"Nobody will ever know what really happened last night. I promise." He gave her another quick kiss before heading out the door.

Under an overhead lamp across the street, the so-called social worker sat in an idling car.

Watching their house.

Chapter Eight

Brad finished off the last of the chicken fried rice, and couldn't help thinking what a sad group they all were. His bruised, stitched, and casted mother sitting next to Hadley, the pregnant teen who'd just killed someone the night before. He and Faye were wiped out from the long night spent dumping a body. Zeke was snipping at everyone. Only Luna was her happy self.

"Can I go upstairs now?" Zeke frowned. "If I don't get more XP, I'm never going to earn that shield before they take it out of the shop."

Faye sighed. "It's only a game. Emptying out that room will bring us more money."

"It isn't *only* a game," Zeke muttered. "And Wynn already got the shield. It's a limited edition."

Hadley glared at him. "Nobody cares."

"Don't be rude," Faye said.

She tilted her head. "You just said that it's only a game."

"But I didn't say nobody cares."

"Whatever." Hadley sighed.

"You're all giving me a headache." Brad pinched his nose. "Zeke, get *your* stuff out of the spare room. That goes for you two, also." He looked at Hadley and Luna. "This is important to your mom, so we're all pitching in. The contractor is coming tomorrow."

"On a Saturday?" Zeke said.

Brad stopped short before turning to Faye. "Did he say tomorrow, or Monday?"

"Tomorrow."

"He's going to be here all weekend?"

She shrugged. "All I know is that he said tomorrow."

"Will it be loud?" Mom asked.

Brad nodded. "Probably. I can take you to your house for a little while if you want."

Her eyes lit up. "Would you?"

"Of course." He rose and picked up the empty plates, his fatigue swallowing him up.

Zeke pushed his chair back. "So, if I get *my* stuff out of the room, I can get back to HardCorps?"

Brad nodded. "Spend the whole night earning XP if you want — as long as you get your junk out of there."

Zeke bolted out of the room.

Hadley set her fork down. "Do I *have* to get my stuff out of there? I'm exhausted."

Brad grabbed a beer from the fridge. "I'll bring it up to your room, but you do have to go through it yourself."

"Thanks, Dad."

"Sure. Get some rest."

"Will do." She yawned and headed upstairs.

"What can I do?" asked his mom.

"You can get some sleep, too."

She shook her head. "I'm not ready. Let me help with the room."

"No. Why don't you settle into your room? I can take

Bingo outside and settle him on your bed. You can watch TV or read. Doesn't that sound nice?"

"Sure." She gave an obviously forced smile. "Thanks, son."

Brad found a bottle opener and guzzled down half a beer. It would take a lot more to soothe his aching muscles, but he didn't have time for that.

He couldn't believe Kurt's contractor was coming over on a Saturday. What kind of strings had Kurt pulled? And why was he so eager to get Brad back to work?

When he got to the spare room, Zeke was muttering as he gathered old toys and sports equipment.

"Are you still complaining?"

"Hadley doesn't have to help."

Brad held back a snappy retort. Zeke had a legitimate complaint. "She isn't feeling well today. She'll still have to deal with her stuff. I'm just going to get it out of here for her. Unless you want to do that."

"No." Zeke narrowed his eyes. "What am I supposed to do with all of this? There isn't space in my room or the garage. That's why it's in here."

"Make a place for it or add it to the donations."

Zeke muttered again before lugging an armful up the stairs.

Faye came in. "How's it going?"

"Zeke's upset about Hadley not pulling her weight."

"He has to understand about her being pregnant."

Brad shook his head. "He's fourteen. All he sees is that he has to do more work than her."

"I'll talk with him."

"I already did."

"Okay." She turned to a bookshelf full of dusty books.

Brad looked around, trying to decide where to start.

Though Faye and Zeke had already emptied out some of the stuff, the room was still packed.

How would they clear it out before the contractor arrived in the morning?

It was going to be another long night. And he wasn't sure he had it in him to pull it off. But he couldn't ask Faye to do all the work.

He returned to the kitchen for another beer. It took the edge off, but didn't make him feel any less sleepy.

He needed coffee. Something stronger than what they had at the house.

Brad went back to the storage room. "I'm going to run out for some coffee. Want one?"

"At this hour?"

"I'll take a mocha," Zeke said. "Extra chocolate and whipped cream."

Brad sighed. "Okay. Faye?"

She rubbed her eyes and looked around the room. "Actually caffeine sounds great. I'll take the strongest thing they have."

"Strongest one available and a mocha. Got it."

"Extra chocolate and whipped cream," Zeke added.

"Anything else? Soy milk, maybe? A flavor?"

Zeke glared at him.

"Be back soon."

But as Brad pulled out onto the street, he saw a familiar car.

The social worker was watching their house again, but this time from an angle they couldn't see from inside any window.

His blood boiled, but there wasn't anything he could do until he could reach an attorney.

That woman either was pretending to be a social worker or she was obsessed with Nate's case for some reason — and either reason made her dangerous. Or at the very least, a major cause for concern.

Brad tried to shove her from his mind, but he couldn't think of anything else as he drove, ordered the coffees, and headed back home.

At least her car was gone when he returned. Brad even drove around the block to make sure. She hadn't followed him, either. He'd checked.

Inside, Faye and Zeke had made impressive progress on the storage room. And with the coffee, the three of them got even more done.

An hour later, Zeke wiped his forehead. "That's all my stuff. Don't yell at me about my room being a mess."

"Nobody's going to yell," Brad said. "But you'll need to figure out what to do with all of that stuff."

"Right now?"

"Soon."

"I can do that. Now I can play my game?"

"Go." Brad waved him off.

Zeke raced up the stairs.

Faye pulled her hair back into a ponytail and looked around. "How are we ever going to get through all of this stuff before Gary arrives tomorrow?"

"The same way we've been doing this — one thing at a time."

"But the desk? The shelves?"

"We'll put them in the entry if we have to. We don't have to figure out where anything goes yet. The only thing that matters is getting it all out, right?"

"As far as Gary's concerned."

"Then that's all we'll worry about for now." Brad hefted a box of books and carried them across the hall to the sitting room.

Two hours later, they'd gotten most of the small stuff out. Only the furniture and a few other items remained.

Faye collapsed onto a swivel chair. "I could sleep for a week."

"You and me both. Do you want to head upstairs?"

"What about this other stuff?"

Brad shrugged. "I'll have Zeke help me with it in the morning."

"Will he be up in time?"

"I guarantee it." He trudged toward the stairs, only to hear cartoons from the living room. "Mom and Luna are still up."

Faye's shoulders dropped. "I'll help your mom into bed if you'll help Luna."

He kissed her. "You're the best."

A full hour later, he finally closed Luna's bedroom door. Somehow, despite Brad's raging fatigue, she'd managed to talk him into reading three stories. It had been hard to refuse, thinking about how quickly Hadley had grown up, and how little time he'd been spending with Luna since Duke's death.

Brad started walking to his room, but stopped. Something sounded in the hall, but he couldn't tell what it was. He spun in a slow circle, unable to identify the noise. Cupped an ear and followed the noise.

Right to Hadley's room. It sounded like sobbing on the other end.

He wasn't sure he could deal with one more thing, but he also couldn't walk away knowing she was crying.

Brad ignored the throbbing pain behind his right temple and knocked.

No response.

He knocked again. "Hadley!"

"Go away."

"I'm coming in." He waited a few beats before opening the door, giving her time to say she had to get dressed or anything else. But she said nothing so he entered.

She sat on her bed, her face red and tear-stained.

"What's the matter?" Brad sat beside her.

"You really have to ask?"

"There's a lot going on. Is it anything in particular?"

"That social worker is on to us! To *me*."

He shook his head. "She's looking into leads. There isn't any reason for her to suspect us."

Hadley gave him an incredulous look.

"There's no evidence pointing toward us. She's grasping at straws."

"But I did it."

"Nobody knows that. So far as anyone knows, Nate's only missing. There isn't a lick of proof of his death."

"But something will come up."

Brad shook his head. "I was careful. Nobody will find anything."

Hadley flipped around and buried her face into the pillow.

He drew a deep breath. "I don't want you worrying about any of this. You need to focus on your health."

She sat up and looked at him like he was crazy. "I killed him."

"It was an accident, and nobody will ever find out."

"Dad, I'm not a four-year-old who swiped a cookie. This is serious."

"I know it is, but so is your health. That's what's important. Let Mom and me handle the rest."

"I should turn myself in."

Her words were a slap to the face. He needed a moment to recover. "What did you just say? I know I didn't hear you correctly."

Her eyes widened. "I need to confess."

"To the cops?"

"Who else?"

"Not a chance."

Tears trailed down her face. "I killed him."

"And your mother and I helped cover it up. You want us to go to jail, too?"

"I won't tell them you helped me."

Brad tugged on his hair. "You're going to tell them you got rid of the body and the blood from the park, all on your own? In one night?"

"Yeah?" It sounded more like a question.

"They won't believe you! We did all of that *so* you wouldn't have to go to jail."

She wiped her eyes. "Don't you see? It was an accident. I didn't mean to do it. He was provoking me. The evidence is on his cell phone. They'll believe me. It'll all be okay, and then his family will know——"

"No!"

Hadley jumped.

"You aren't telling anyone anything. Do you understand me?"

"But——"

"There is no *but*. None! We're already deep into this. Think about this. If we all go to jail, what will happen to Luna and Zeke? Grandma?"

Her mouth gaped.

"Exactly. Your time to confess was right after you killed him. But you didn't go to the cops. You came to us. Brought us in. Now we're as guilty as you are by covering it all up. You can't do this to your family."

"Like I said, I'll say I did it all."

"And you expect them to believe that a pregnant teenager pulled all of this off by herself?"

Hadley stared at him.

"Tell me, how did you move the body? Hide it? And then clean up all the blood?"

She shook her head.

"You can't. This is another secret you're going to have to keep — just like your relationship with Duke."

"Which everyone knows about now."

"But nobody knew anything during the investigation."

She buried her face in her palms and mumbled something.

"You're going to keep quiet … is that what you said?"

Hadley looked up at him. "I can't live like this."

"You're going to have to. You've made some very adult decisions lately, and there are serious consequences."

More tears welled in her eyes.

"Think about that baby of yours — your one tie to Duke. What do you think will happen to it?" Brad hated using that logic, but his options were few.

He had to keep her from talking to the police.

She sniffled. "I could still adopt it out."

"And how do you think carrying a baby in prison will work out? Do you realize how inmates treat each other? You'll miscarry in a month."

Hadley gasped.

"I'm just telling you the truth. If you think prisoners are nice people, you're living in a fantasy world."

"But it was an accident."

"Do you have any idea how many inmates claim innocence?"

"But I *am*!"

He lifted a brow.

"It was an accident."

"But you killed him, right?"

She looked away.

"That isn't something the police will simply overlook. Or the judge or jury."

Her face paled.

"This is serious stuff, Hadley. You can't just say you're sorry and you didn't mean to, then carry on with your life. *Maybe* if you'd called them from the park as he was still bleeding, if you'd tried to save him while you waited for an ambulance. But more than twenty-four hours later? After hiding the body and destroying evidence? No way."

She leaped up from the bed and ran out of the room.

Brad followed her into the hall.

Retching sounded from the bathroom.

Hadley returned a few minutes later.

"Did you have a chance to think about it?" he asked.

She chewed on her lower lip.

"Well?"

"You really think all that will happen? I'll go to jail and the real criminals will be mean to me?"

"Mean? You'll be lucky if that's all they are. People will assault you. I can promise you that."

"How do you know?"

"I've lived a whole lot longer than you and seen a whole lot more."

"But girl prisoners will be nicer."

Brad snorted. "Dream on."

She looked even more deflated.

He put his arm around her. "It's late, and we're both tired. Let's get some sleep."

"Okay."

He helped her settle back into bed. "One more thing."

"What?"

"I'm going to take your electronics."

"Why?" she exclaimed.

"I don't want you confessing to anyone."

"But I won't."

"That's not a risk I'm willing to take at this point." He held out his hand.

"Dad, please."

"Phone, tablet, and laptop."

She shook her head.

"You won't need them while you sleep, anyway."

After another minute of back and forth, she handed them over.

"You'll thank me for this later."

Hadley glared at her father as he closed the door.

Chapter Nine

Brad waved to Gary, then closed the door and turned to Faye. "This is crazy."

"It's happening so fast. I should give my notice at the salon." Her eyes brightened with excitement.

Brad rubbed the back of his aching neck and tried to smile. It was hard, given that he was even more tired today than yesterday. He'd been plagued with dreams of Hadley turning herself into the police. Fortunately, she'd done no such thing.

"Where should we start?" Faye looked at the mostly empty room. "The shelves?"

"Hold on. Before you talk to your boss, think about leaving yourself enough time to let your clients know you're starting your own business."

"I hope I'm allowed to tell them. There's so much to think about."

"Don't worry about what they want you to say. Just tell your clients. You can't help it if they ask for more information, and you should certainly give it to them if they do. It's easier to ask for forgiveness than permission."

"Maybe."

"Definitely. But let's take this one thing at a time. We need to clear out this furniture before Gary comes back with his crew."

They got the room emptied in record time, but there was no place to sit in their sitting room and they had to turn sideways to get through the hall. At least the entry was unwelcoming to anyone wanting to stop by and ask questions. That was one benefit to the mess.

As everyone was finishing lunch, the doorbell rang.

Faye rushed to answer it before the ringing stopped.

Hadley pushed her plate away. "At least she can be happy about something when there's so much else going on."

"Having her salon here will benefit all of us." Brad pushed his chair out. "Let's support your mother."

"I have a headache. I'm going to take a nap." Hadley took her things to the sink and sulked away.

"What's with her?" Zeke asked. "I mean, besides the usual."

Brad yawned. "She's under a lot of pressure. We all are."

Zeke didn't look like he believed him. "I'm getting back to HardCorps. Still trying to catch up on my XP from last night. I'm going to be lucky to get enough in time."

Brad took his plate to the sink and went to the nearest bathroom to find some ibuprofen. Or even something stronger. The pounding in his head wouldn't give up. He was tempted to follow Hadley's lead and go back to bed. But he needed to meet Gary's crew and be there with Faye as they started. And at some point, Kurt would expect him to come back to work.

It was nearly an hour later when the construction began. Even upstairs in his room with earplugs in, he could still hear the noise. He pulled the pillow over his head, but that didn't help, either.

And the crew hadn't been able to give him an estimate on how long the project would take. This could go on for the next week. Or longer.

He tried to sleep despite the pounding, which battled with his headache, but it was pointless. Even with his fatigue, he couldn't get a nap.

Knock, knock!

Didn't everyone know he was trying to sleep?

Knock, knock, knock!

"Come in." He pulled out his earplugs.

The door flung open, and Hadley marched in without closing it behind her, making the construction noise even louder. "I can't sleep."

"Either can I, obviously."

"How long are they going to be doing that?"

"Until Mom's salon is ready." Brad sat up. "If it gets bad enough, we can go to Grandma's house."

"Whatever. Can I get my phone back?"

"What for?"

"Because it's mine."

"That doesn't answer my question."

"I can't sleep, and I need to know what people are saying about Nate."

"Nothing new. I already checked. People are wondering what happened to him, but so far people seem to think he ran away."

"Nobody thinks he was murdered?"

Brad sighed. "He wasn't *murdered*."

"I know, but people could think that."

"Don't worry about what anyone is saying."

"How can I not? I was arguing with him after school. I'm the obvious suspect."

"Nobody thinks you're a killer. Go take your nap."

"I can't. Not with all this racket. At least let me have my phone so I can scroll. It'll make me sleepier."

He shook his head. "If you want to make yourself tired, read a book. I have a few that will knock you out in no time."

"Ugh. Seriously?"

"Yes."

Her brows furrowed as she stared at him, but then Hadley spun around and left, leaving the door wide open.

Brad stared, wanting to close it, but his fatigue was winning out. He fell back onto the pillow and replaced the earplugs.

Faye walked in, closed the door, and said something.

He took the plugs out. "What?"

"Why did Hadley just slam her door?"

"Because I wouldn't give her phone back."

"You still think she'll turn herself in?" Faye sat next to him.

"We can't risk it."

"What about her tablet or laptop? She can't make calls through those."

"She could post her confession. I need to be sure she won't do anything rash. And after hearing her last night, it'll be a while before I feel good about that."

A strange expression crossed Faye's face.

"What?"

"Nothing."

He sat up again. "That wasn't nothing."

"I had a thought, but you won't like it."

"What is it?"

"Like I said, you won't like it."

"Just tell me. I don't feel like playing games."

She hesitated.

"I already have a raging headache. Please don't make it worse than it already is."

"Maybe we should tell her about your line of work."

"You mean what I *really* do?"

Faye nodded.

A new pain shot through the top of his head. "Get me more ibuprofen."

"Brad—"

"I'm serious. I'm not going to be able to function. I need more."

"How much have you already taken?"

"Two, three. I don't know. Would you get it for me? Or do I need to get it myself?" He flung off the covers.

"Those aren't good for your stomach."

"I'll deal with that later. First, the headache."

She sighed. "I wasn't trying to upset you. If you'd hear me out—"

"I'll get it myself." He swung his feet off the bed.

"Let me." Faye disappeared into their bathroom and made noise as she dug through the cabinet. She returned with two tiny tablets and a little paper cup.

"Thanks." He would get some more later.

After he swallowed the pills, Faye sat next to him again. "Will you hear me out?"

"Have at it. Let's hear your reasoning for wanting to tell a doubly-hormonal teenager my life-threatening secret."

She gave him an exasperated look.

"Well?"

"Are you going to hear me out?"

"That's what I'm doing, isn't it?"

Faye took a deep breath. "Hadley is beside herself with worry about being caught. She's also wracked with guilt."

"All completely understandable. The guilt is a good sign."

She lifted a brow.

"If our daughter killed someone and didn't care, we'd have a whole different set of problems to deal with."

"That's true. But we can take some of the load off her by letting her know you know what you're doing."

Brad pushed his pillows up to the headboard and leaned against them. "I've already told her that multiple times."

"But she sees you as her dad, a knife salesman. Not … a trained assassin."

"You obviously have a hard time with it. Do you think it'll be any easier for Hadley to handle? She already has enough on her plate."

"At least she'll be able to rest assured that the body won't be found. That'll take a big burden off her mind."

"I've already told her as much."

Faye looked deep in thought for a moment. "But it would mean so much more if she knew that you do this every day."

"Not every day."

"You know what I mean."

Brad rubbed his temples again. They were even more tender than before. "What if she can't see the difference between assassin and serial killer? She could think I'm a criminal, or worse, a psychopath. I'm neither."

"Obviously. I'm sure she'll understand the difference."

"*I'm* not convinced Hadley will grasp it. The news was a lot for you to take in, and you're neither a teenager nor pregnant."

"What does that have to do with anything?"

"You're a mature adult. Her brain is still developing,

not to mention the insane amount of hormones racing through her."

"Would you stop talking about the hormones? It's getting old."

"No. It's a valid point, and you're talking about telling her top secret information. What if she lets it slip to one of her friends? To the therapist? The police? None of these people can know what I do."

"But our daughter is talking about turning herself in."

"And that's precisely why I took her electronics."

"You don't think she could find another way if she really wanted?"

"It's an extra step she'd have to take. She'll have to think about everything I told her."

Faye took his hand. "I don't want to see her spiral, and I know you don't either. If we tell her this one thing, she can rest easy and not burst into tears every time the doorbell rings."

Brad closed his eyes. "I don't want my girl looking at me like I'm a heartless killer."

Faye squeezed his hand. "Honey, she just killed her friend. What she needs is someone who will understand. You can talk about how you felt the first time you took a life. That's not something I can do, or Dr. Trellis, or anyone else. You're the only one who can help her, and in order to get her through this, she has to know what you do. You don't have to tell her everything — leave out sensitive information, but tell her what you can."

He opened his eyes. "That does make sense. Let me think about how to open that can of worms."

She wrapped her arms around him. "You'll really do this?"

"I still have my reservations, but she does need someone to talk to about this. And I'm the only one who's been there. You're right about that helping her. And if she doesn't know I've been through it myself, she probably won't listen to me."

Faye rose. "Let's go talk to her."

"Now? No. I need to think about this. This has to be handled delicately. I need to know exactly what I'm going to say before I speak with her."

"But you'll do it? Today?"

"Just give me some space to figure this all out."

She squeezed him.

"Another thing. We're going to have to coach her on how to keep this quiet. The police and that social worker will be asking more, not less, questions. We can't risk her accidentally saying anything."

"I'll help however I can." Faye gave him a big smile.

Hopefully he was making the right decision.

If not, all three of them could end up in jail.

ZACHARY CLARK AND AMY MCELROY FISHER

Chapter Ten

"BE BACK IN ABOUT TWENTY." Zeke turned off his mic and placed his headset on the desk. He wanted to play another round, but he couldn't ignore his growling stomach another moment.

He stepped into the hallway. The noise from downstairs was even louder out here. At least he couldn't hear any of it while working on his game. He needed all his attention on earning XP. It was hard with so many people playing for the tournament. Basically everyone with an account was on this weekend. At least the inactives were easy kills.

Downstairs, the pounding, thumping, and whacking was even louder. It made his ears ring in the kitchen. He dug through the fridge and freezer, settling on frozen burritos, and plugged his ears while they turned in the microwave.

Once back upstairs, he stopped before going into his room. All the other bedroom doors were closed, except Luna's. His parents and Hadley were still acting weird. His sister was only coming out of her room for meals, and barely saying anything. It was still strange enough that she wasn't constantly out with her friends, though she was probably still depressed over Duke.

If he was being honest with himself, it was still mind-blowing that the next-door neighbor who had been mentoring him on how to deal with the bullies at school had also been with his sister at the same time. Although, maybe that was why Duke had taken such an interest in him — his girlfriend's kid brother.

Otherwise, Zeke would've been invisible to him, just like he was to everyone else. Either that or the butt of jokes.

Not that any of that mattered now. He needed to know what his family was hiding — and of course Hadley was in the middle. She got away with everything.

She was probably getting away with something *right now*. The thought boiled his blood.

He marched down the hall and pressed his ear to the door. Could only make out a few faint notes of music, and even that was hard to hear over the construction downstairs. Even if she wasn't *doing* something wrong, she was probably either plotting something or in the process of covering something up. There was zero doubt about that.

Zeke plugged his other ear, but still couldn't hear anything. It wasn't fair that she got away with everything *and* that people loved her so much. But that was probably why the world practically revolved around her.

And yet here he was with almost all of the same DNA, and he was a freak who could get in trouble for crossing his arms or rolling his eyes.

He wanted to burst into her room and yell at her, but what good would that do? He'd just get in trouble. She'd probably dissolve into tears for added effect.

At least she'd be out of the house before too long. Then

he wouldn't have to compete with her. Not that he tried. He got low grades and didn't do sports — he was a run-of-the-mill underachiever — because what was the point when Hadley Morris was his sister? Having everyone look at him like he was a joke was better than trying the impossible task of living up to her. It was kind of nice not having anyone expect anything of him.

Even though he could do more. Plenty more. If he *wanted*, he could get stellar grades. The fact that he was better at HardCorps than any of his friends proved that much. He'd put his mind to that. But nobody cared.

Maybe if he was able to be one of those millionaire video game YouTubers, people would take notice. Realize he was actually good at it.

Good at something.

Even if they didn't think it mattered. It took talent to reach the top tiers that he'd achieved. Casual players didn't even come close. Even people who threw thousands of dollars every month to skip through the levels didn't reach where Zeke got most seasons.

He balled his fists and marched down the hall.

His parents' voices drifted from their room.

It wasn't like they cared about anything that was important to him. But the people on the other end of the computer screen and his earphones did.

They were impressed with him, the things he'd accomplished.

Once in his room, he pushed his dresser against the door and opened the coffee tin that he'd labeled *Video Game Tips* assuring nobody would touch it. And they hadn't. He'd rigged it with a hair that would've fallen off at the slightest tampering.

Set the hair aside, pulled off the lid, and breathed in the scent of mixed long-ago used coffee and cold hard cash. It was better than a fresh-cooked meal after hours without eating.

He pulled out the stacks of cash he'd been saving for years. When he earned his allowance or wages for mowing neighbors' lawns or whatever, most of it went in here. Some went to HardCorps, but most got poured into his savings. Sure, he could put it in the bank and earn almost nothing in interest. But this was gold for one reason.

Nobody knew anything about it.

And now he had almost everything he needed. Maybe he had it all by now.

He went to his wallet, pulled out the wad of bills, and yanked off the rubber bands. Mrs. Miller, the widowed cat lady down the street, had recently paid Zeke a near fortune for clearing out her gutters and weeding. Granted, it had been quite the job, with all those leaves and pine needles that had piled up, but he hadn't expected *that* much. But with everything going on at home, he hadn't added the new money to his collection.

His heart raced as he unrolled each bill and added them up. Counted a second and third time to be sure he'd gotten it right. Logged it. Calculated the new total.

He had enough. He finally earned what he needed to buy all of the equipment he needed to run a pro channel. The expensive mic with all the doodads, the editing software, and the hundred other things that nobody ever thought of.

But Zeke had done his research. And knew every little thing needed.

Now he could take his cash and buy one of those credit card gift cards to buy it all online. Then he'd just have to wait for everything to arrive.

While he waited, he'd set up his channel. He already had the account, just hadn't done anything with it yet.

His heart hammered. More than anything, he wanted to tell his parents of his accomplishment.

But he couldn't say a word. They wouldn't understand. Not even close. And worse, they might even try to talk him out of it, or even go as far as forbidding it.

He would stay quiet. He'd managed this long. Besides, the real thrill would be growing his following and his income. His parents would be impressed, once he was making more than them.

Not even Hadley would be able to steal his limelight.

He just needed to get himself to a store that sold the cards.

He was so close to posting his first pro video. Too bad none of it would arrive in time for him to start with this weekend's event. He was already killing it, despite the hours lost to cleaning out that room downstairs.

Zeke put his cash into his backpack, zipped it up, and rested it against his desk. His heart thrummed in his ears, even blocking out the sounds of the construction.

Hands shaking, he replaced his dresser and marched back into the hall, feeling ten feet tall. Knocked on his parents' door to ask them for a ride.

It pushed open.

He stepped inside the dim room.

Empty.

His heart sank. Had they left?

No. They wouldn't go without telling him. Nobody had said a word.

Zeke checked the other rooms. All empty. Except Hadley's.

He didn't knock. Didn't want to look at her face if he didn't have to. Went downstairs. Only found Grandma and Luna. They were outside with Bingo, Grandma's dog. He couldn't blame them with all the noise.

His parents had either gone somewhere or were in Hadley's room.

They were with his sister.

That meant he would have to see her if he wanted to ask them anything. Normally, he'd just wait. But this wasn't any ordinary time.

He had the money to order all of his equipment. Just needed to get to the store, get his gift card, and order the items. Then he could get back to the HardCorps event and still get the in-game items.

Zeke hurried to his sister's room. Hesitated before knocking. Stopped himself. If he knocked, she could tell him to go away. Push him out. Or their parents, if they were in there, could send him back to his room.

But not if he caught them all off guard. Zeke could tell them what he needed, and possibly get one of them to agree to drive him. Maybe even Hadley. He wanted a ride so much, he didn't even care if she was the one to take him.

He turned the knob, half-expecting it to be locked. But it opened right up and Zeke practically fell inside.

"—And I'm actually an assassin." Dad stopped talking.

Zeke skidded to a stop, eyes wide.

Expecting the punchline.

None came.

Everyone else's eyes were as wide as his.

He looked at his dad. "Did you just say you're an assassin?"

Dad pointed to the door. "Go to your room. Now!"

Zeke ran.

Chapter Eleven

BRAD STARED in disbelief at the door. How had Zeke chosen that exact moment to burst into the room?

It wasn't bad enough that he'd agreed to tell Hadley, but back in his room or not, now Zeke knew, too.

He should've gone with his gut and told Faye no.

Their teenage children did not need this information.

Yet they both had it now.

Hadley at least didn't have access to the internet.

Zeke, however, had it all.

"Brad?" Faye was pale as a sheet.

He looked back and forth between his wife and daughter.

Hadley's eyes looked like they could pop out of her head. "*Did* you say you're an assassin? Like, for real?"

"It's true."

"An assassin? A trained killer? You." She shook her head.

"Is it *really* that hard to believe?"

"Come on, Dad. You live in a typical suburban neighborhood with three kids. You sell knives."

"I teach people knife safety. I'm a weapons expert."

She shook her head. "That's crazy talk."

Every muscle in his body tensed. "I'm telling you the truth. I've been dealing with dead bodies for years. My livelihood depends on it." He glanced toward the hall again before turning back to her. "I'm only telling you because I need you to trust me when I say nobody will find Nate. This is top secret information. You can't tell anyone. Do you understand?"

Hadley nodded slowly. She didn't look like she believed him.

He didn't have time to convince her.

"As long as you don't breathe a word of this to anyone. I need to talk to your brother." He glanced at Faye. "I need you to answer her questions. Can you do that?"

"Yes. What are you going to say to Zeke?"

"I'm going tell him that he misheard — that his mind is on video games. I need you two to play along if he asks. Got it?"

They both nodded.

"Good." He put his hand on Hadley's. "And what I need from you is to stop worrying about getting caught. It isn't going to happen. I won't let it, and I have the experience to make sure nobody ever suspects you. Do you trust me?"

"I guess."

"You *guess*?"

"You have to admit this is all totally crazy."

He drew a deep breath. "This is *serious*. I know what I'm doing, and I'm going to make sure you don't get caught. Do you understand?"

Hadley swallowed. "Yes."

"Are you sure?"

"I am."

He let a beat pass before responding. "I won't let anything happen to you." He hurried out of the room, closing the door behind him. The last thing they needed was for anyone else in the house to overhear the discussion of Brad's job.

But his first priority was to convince Zeke he'd heard wrong.

Shouldn't be that hard.

Except that his son was sharp. He tried to play it off that he wasn't, but Brad could see through the act. His son tried *not* to try. He'd long ago tired of attempting to live up to his sister.

Brad couldn't underestimate the kid.

It would be no easy task convincing him that he'd misheard. He was kidding himself if he thought otherwise.

Knock, knock!

"Go away!"

"It's me," Brad called.

"I said, go away!"

Brad drew a deep breath. "We need to talk."

"No, we don't."

"I'm coming in." He waited for an objection.

Didn't get one, so he marched in.

Zeke was at his desk, his headphones on. The screensaver was on his computer.

"We need to talk."

No response.

Brad closed the door and stood by the desk. "Did you say you thought I said I was an assassin?"

"I can't hear you."

"Yes, you can."

"No, I don't."

Brad pulled off the headset. "What do you think you heard in there?"

"Think? You said you're an assassin?"

"Why would you think I said that?"

"Because that's what you *said*." Zeke turned to him, his expression unreadable.

"An assassin?" Brad forced a laugh. "You misheard me. Why would I say that?"

"Then what did you say?"

He should've had that ready before he'd come in here. His only choice was to deflect. "Do I look like an assassin to you?"

Zeke crossed his arms.

"I'm a knife salesman. And according to you, a dorky one at that."

"And you've been suspected of murdering two people this year." Zeke narrowed his eyes.

"I didn't kill Duke or Allison. Their real killers are now in jail. You'll notice I'm free — because I didn't do it."

Silence settled between them as Zeke stared him down.

"Think about it, Zeke. *Your* dad, an assassin. Really? That's crazy talk."

"Then why are you in here trying to convince me you're not one?"

"Do you hear yourself?"

"You know, it actually makes sense." He leaned forward, holding Brad's gaze.

"How so?"

"It explains all your traveling. The 'conventions.'" Zeke made air quotes when he said it. "I mean seriously, how many knife shows could there be in one year? Not as many as you supposedly go to."

Brad clenched his jaw. It was just his luck that the kid he *didn't* want knowing he was an assassin did believe him, while the one he needed to trust him, didn't.

"See? You can't even argue the point."

Brad's mind raced. He had to do something. But what?

What he really needed was some time to think about how to handle this.

"How long have you been killing people?"

Brad stared at him. "You can't believe that's what I do?"

"Why not?"

"I knew it was a bad idea letting you play so many video games."

"What?" Zeke exclaimed.

"Now you think it's no big deal for me to be an alleged assassin."

His faced reddened. "That has nothing to do with my games. It's putting everything together. It *makes sense*. It's called logical thinking."

"I'm sure your teachers would be proud."

Zeke scowled.

"Would you be in here trying to convince me if it wasn't true? You'd be rolling your eyes, not bothering with me. The fact that you're so worried tells me I'm right. Deny it."

Brad knelt to meet his son at his sitting eye level. "I am not an assassin."

"Is that part of your training? You always told *me* not to lie."

"You think I'd lie to you?"

"You're doing it right now."

Brad swore.

Zeke sat there with a smug expression.

Should he continue denying, or go with it? Faye was already in Hadley's room, coaching her on what to say and how to deal with the news. He would have to do the same with Zeke. It'd be easier to drag his son in there and deal with both kids at once, but he couldn't risk Zeke finding out about Hadley killing Nate.

Brad had to keep them separated until they both grew used to the news of his being an assassin.

Good thing his headache had disappeared. There was no way he could handle all of this with his brain like a punching bag.

"Well?" Zeke stared at him expectantly.

The construction noise seemed to grow louder. Made it harder to think.

"You gonna admit the truth?"

Brad stormed toward the door. "Get your coat and shoes."

Zeke's face lost color. "What do you mean?"

"Exactly what I said."

"Where are we going?"

"You'll find out when we get there."

"Dad?"

"Now." Brad narrowed his eyes. "Be downstairs in no more than two minutes."

"But—"

He closed the door between them and checked on Faye and Hadley.

They were deep in conversation.

He left, not wanting to interrupt. In the meantime, he needed to figure out where he and Zeke were going. It had to be somewhere far enough that he would have time to think in the car, but close enough that they could get back home as soon as possible.

Brad knew exactly where to take him. The perfect place to talk in privacy.

And with any luck, he could find a few answers for himself.

Chapter Twelve

BRAD GRABBED a few things from his room to take to his mom's house, away from anyone nosy who might sneak around the house during construction hours. Then he checked to make sure his office was locked. He paused, his hand still on the knob.

He needed to return to his father's office to look through more of his things. Though he'd gotten enough to prove to himself that Dad had been involved with the same car wash assassin ring as Wes, he needed more.

If his dad had left more clues behind, Brad would find them.

He would take Zeke to his mom's house and figure out what to do on the way there. If he needed more time, he'd think while going through his dad's things.

It was the perfect timing. If he rifled through the room while his mom was there, she'd want to be there with him.

That wasn't going to happen. No way he was going to let his ailing mother find out that her husband had been an assassin. She'd be crushed — and learning that her son was also one could do her in completely.

Going to her house now was the ideal solution.

Zeke paced at the front door, tugging on his hair, as Brad came downstairs. He followed his father to the car without a peep.

Brad started the engine. "Not a word."

His son gave him a side-eyed glance but stayed silent.

After pulling out of the neighborhood, Brad relaxed a little. His mind raced. Did he dare admit the truth? There would be no going back. And it'd be a lot harder to coach Zeke than Hadley. He was harder to not only control but predict.

Not that he had any control over his daughter — that much was obvious. But Zeke was … Zeke. Wild at his core.

But he was already convinced that Brad was an assassin. And this car ride wasn't likely to convince him otherwise.

Unless Zeke changed his tune by the time they reached Mom's house, Brad would have to shoot straight with him. Admit that he was actually a trained killer. Then he would have to lay down the law. Make sure his son understood the magnitude of such knowledge. Teach him how to handle it.

After all these years of raising his kids to be honest, now he needed to teach them to lie. Or at the very least, how to avoid giving away his secret.

It was a matter of life and death. National security. In the hands of his teenagers.

How had it come down to this?

He needed to get this under control, and fast.

Amazingly, his son stayed quiet for the ride over. He threw Brad a questioning glance once inside.

Brad locked the door. "Follow me."

He led Zeke to the office and pointed to a chair near the door. One his own dad had made him sit at numerous times growing up. He shoved those thoughts aside. Went to a file cabinet he'd been wanting to go through, pulled out the top drawer, and looked at the labels on files.

A few minutes passed in silence. He got to the back of the top drawer, finding nothing interesting. Not that his dad would've labeled any of them *assassinations*. Brad would most likely have to go through all of the papers individually.

From the corner of his eye he could see Zeke starting to fidget. He would have to start talking soon. His son was probably going crazy, wondering what Brad would do or say when he finally spoke.

First, he wanted to find something in his dad's things. Proof that would link BlueBlade to the Slippery Fish. The two were connected, despite Kurt's claims to the contrary. The only people who could help draw the lines were either dead or not talking. Wes was in jail after trying to pin Allison's murder on Brad. Kurt wouldn't admit the truth without undeniable proof — and Brad needed to find that within these walls.

He slammed the drawer shut and moved down to the next one, checking each file label as quickly as possible. As he was getting to the back of the second drawer, he was about ready to call it a day. He couldn't leave Faye at home to deal with everything there much longer.

Brad started to slam the drawer shut when he noticed a file jammed down in the back. He yanked up, ripping part of it.

He stopped, then angled himself and pulled more gingerly. It tore slightly more before coming loose.

It was labeled *Car Wash*.

Brad's heart hammered. This was something. But what?

Whatever it was, it would have to wait.

He set it on the desk and stood in front of Zeke. "What are you thinking?"

"I don't know."

"Don't give me that."

"How can you be an assassin? You've always told us how important it is to be honest, but you've been lying to us this whole time."

Zeke had him there. But he couldn't let his son know that. "I've been telling you as much as I could. Now you know something you shouldn't."

"Why'd you tell Hadley? Do you trust her more than me?"

Brad paced. "There are extenuating circumstances that led to us needing to tell her. I didn't want to, but it was necessary."

"Why? Because she's pregnant?"

"Because of things that have nothing to do with you."

"The pregnancy?"

"Obviously not." Brad stopped his pacing in front of Zeke. "But you weren't supposed to overhear that, either. How is it you keep ending up finding out things you aren't meant to know?"

"I'm observant."

Pressure built behind his eyes. The last thing he needed was for his headache to return. He pinched the top of his nose and thought about what to say before looking at his son. "Do you understand how serious it is that you stay silent about this?"

Zeke swallowed. "Are you going to have to kill me?"

Brad froze in place. "What?"

"Now that I know, do you have to kill me?"

He nearly laughed at the absurdity. "Of course not. You're my son. I'd never hurt you."

"What's going on, then?" Zeke demanded. "If you

don't have to kill me, why bring me here? Why act all secretive? And what does Grandpa's office have to do with anything?"

"Because we needed to get out of the house," he snapped. "Somewhere quiet."

"Why were you going through those drawers? What's in the file?"

"Nothing that concerns you." Brad stepped closer. "The only thing you need to worry about is staying quiet about all of this."

"You think anyone would believe me if I told them?"

"This isn't a joke!"

Zeke jolted. "Okay."

"This is the furthest thing from a joke you could imagine. You don't breathe a word of this to anyone. Ever."

"Got it."

"Not to Wynn, not to anyone."

"What about Hadley?"

Brad narrowed his eyes. "This is serious!"

"Exactly why I'm asking. She knows, too."

"The best thing would be to forget you ever found out."

"Like that's going to happen."

Brad brought his dad's chair around the desk and sat knee-to-knee with his son. "Listen to me. I'm only going to say this once."

Zeke nodded, eyes wide.

"The security clearance needed for this information is high. Not even the police know about me or my bosses."

"Is Kurt your real boss, or is he a—"

"The less you know the better. We need to discuss what you'll say if anyone ever asks about any of this."

Zeke sat up straight. "I'll tell them you're a boring knife salesman. My dad's as dull as they come."

"How many times must I repeat myself? This is not a joke."

"I'm being serious."

"Things get dicey. You should be aware of that — I've been accused of two murders this year alone. And I couldn't say anything about my job to Detective Stewart, because she can't know. Do you have any idea what it's like to walk that line?"

Zeke frowned and shook his head.

"And now you might have to do just that, because you know the truth."

"I won't tell anyone, Dad. I swear. That's the last thing I'd ever want. Sure, I get mad at you for things, but why would I want you going to jail? Look what happened to Nate."

Brad's insides turned to ice. "What do you mean?"

"He's so upset, he ran away. I thought he was so put together, but I guess it's even too much for him. He seemed like the kind of guy who would be there to take care of his younger brother and sister. You never know how stress will affect someone, apparently."

"Right." Brad squared his shoulders. "That's why we need to go over this now."

"Go over what?"

Brad drew a deep breath and held it a moment. "Go over what you'll say if anyone questions you."

"Oh, yeah. Like I said, I'll talk about the knife shop. That's your cover, right?"

"Yes. But if someone puts on pressure—"

"I'm not going to say anything!" Zeke's eyes held hurt. "I'd lie before letting anyone take you away. Why don't you trust me?"

"Because it can be hard enough for an adult. You're barely a teenager."

"I'm going to be fifteen soon. You make it sound like I just turned thirteen."

Brad's phone buzzed with a text. Faye was probably wondering where they were. "My point is, it's a lot of pressure to put on someone your age. I didn't even want to put that on your mother. Yet here we are — now you and your sister know, too."

"You can trust me."

"It's other people I don't trust." Brad rubbed his temples. "People who will make threats. Men and women who will torture someone to get the truth out of them."

"You think someone would torture me?" Zeke's voice squeaked a little.

"If they thought you knew something they needed to know."

"I don't know what you're talking about."

"Good." Brad nodded in approval. "That's convincing. But could you keep it up if someone threatened Luna?"

Zeke went pale. "What?"

"Could you remain just as convincing?"

"What kind of monster would threaten her?"

"Rose."

"From your work?"

"Yeah. She kidnapped Luna and held her at Duke's house to try and trap me."

"She seemed so nice."

"Nice. Right." Brad snorted. "Looks can be deceiving."

"Wait. She's an assassin, too? Is everyone you work with?"

"Yes, she was an assassin, and no, most of the store's employees are salespeople. But we need to focus. Let's pretend Detective Stewart shows up and starts questioning you."

"About what?"

"Anything! It doesn't matter. I could be accused of murder again. Maybe they want to know where Nate went. Just go along with me."

Zeke chewed on his lip, but he nodded.

"You're minding your own business. Walking Bingo at the park, then out of nowhere the detective shows up and starts asking you a bunch of questions. What do you do?"

"Uh, tell her to call your lawyer?"

"That's a good start. You shouldn't say anything without legal representation. What if she says she just has a few questions? That she needs your help, and that it doesn't involve me?"

"I'll tell her I know my rights?"

Brad wrung his hands together. "I sure hope you don't say all of that as a question when speaking to any cop."

"I won't."

"You'd better not. If you don't sound sure of yourself, they'll pounce. No question."

Brad's phone buzzed again.

"We'd better get back home. For now, focus on lawyering up if anyone says anything to you. But we'll have to spend more time talking about this. Maybe even have a mini seminar with you and your sister."

Zeke sighed dramatically. "Awesome."

Brad held his gaze. "As long as you understand the seriousness of this."

"I do."

"You'd better. Our lives are on the line."

Chapter Thirteen

ZEKE STAYED at the window for a full two minutes after his dad's car disappeared from sight, hands shaking.

Was Dad leaving to kill someone? Or did he have other important assassination business to take care of? Maybe going back to Grandpa's office to dig around through the files again?

Or he could be doing something boring like picking up breakfast or going to BlueBlade to sell knives.

It was so weird knowing that was only a cover. For killing people.

And now Zeke knew something that not even the police had the clearance to know.

How crazy was that?

It almost felt unreal. Seriously, how could his dad be a killer? It hardly seemed possible, yet it was true. Dad had *flipped* the night before. Dragging him to Grandma's house and staying quiet so long.

Zeke had thought he would wet himself. He hadn't known what Dad would do.

It was enough to make Zeke want to sneak back over

there and go through that office himself. But it was too far to walk and he didn't have a key.

Maybe he could convince Hadley to drive. And if she didn't have a key either, they could bring Grandma along. She'd be happy to spend some time in her own home.

For that to work, he needed to get on Hadley's good side. Not that it was a bad idea anyway. He still needed to find out why Dad thought she needed to know about him being an assassin.

Ideas ran wild, but he was wasting time. Especially with needing to get more XP for his game. Though admittedly, that didn't seem as important now.

His dad was a killer.

Zeke wandered down the hallway, his mind racing. In a matter of one weekend, his family had gone from boringly normal to insanely interesting. Did anyone else have massive secrets? His dad and sister were hiding things — what about his mom? Grandma? If she knew something, she might've forgotten. Maybe that was why Dad had been going through the office.

He stopped outside Hadley's room. It was quiet. Or maybe he couldn't hear anything over the sounds of construction. It seemed like the crew had barely stopped for the night before starting again this morning.

Hopefully, they'd be done soon. He didn't know how much longer he could put up with it. But then the new annoyance would be Mom's clients. Would they ring the doorbell at all hours? Or had Mom said something about a different entrance? It was hard to remember. He hadn't thought it would happen any time soon, so he hadn't paid attention.

Zeke knocked, but not too loudly. If he wanted Hadley's cooperation, he couldn't risk pissing her off. And waking her would surely do just that.

"Come in," she called.

He shook off his surprise — she probably didn't realize it was him — and entered.

She glared at him from her bed. "What do you want?"

"Do you know where Dad went?"

"No."

"Aren't you even slightly curious?"

She shrugged. "Why would I be?"

He closed the door behind him and hurried over to her. "What if he's killing someone right now?"

"In broad daylight? Seriously?"

Zeke frowned. "What else would he be doing this early on a Sunday morning?"

"Going to church."

"Right. He kills people on Saturday nights, then goes to church on Sundays."

"Why not? It would clear a guilty conscience."

"He doesn't seem to feel too bad about it."

Hadley threw him a frustrated look. "Is there something else you want?"

He studied her. "Why did he tell you about being an assassin?"

"Because he did."

"That's not an answer."

"Did you ask him?"

"You're so frustrating!" Zeke glared at her. "Why did he tell you?"

"I have a lot on my plate, so you can leave."

"You aren't better than everyone else, you know."

Her brows twitched. "Obviously. Why are you pointing that out?"

"Because it sure seems that way! You're walking around with secrets between you and our parents, and you get away with everything."

"You don't have any clue what you're talking about."

"Don't I?"

"You already know I'm pregnant and my boyfriend is dead." Her voice cracked. "What else do you want from me?"

"And Dad told you a government secret because of *that*?"

"Does he work for the government?"

Zeke leaned against the dresser and folded his arms. "Sure sounded that way to me."

She got up and pulled on a fluffy bathrobe. "I didn't get that impression."

"He told me his job is secret from even the police. Something about needing clearance. Sounds like he works for the government."

"Or maybe they're rogue and have to stay off everyone's radar. Then we're back to him needing penance on Sundays."

"You really think so?"

Hadley shrugged. "All I know is what Mom told me about keeping this quiet. Think you can do that?"

"Yes. Can you?"

"I know how to keep a secret."

"You saying I don't?" he countered.

"I'm *saying* I can. Isn't it obvious? Nobody had any idea about Duke and me."

Zeke took a deep breath. Coming in here to talk with her had been pointless. "So, if even you did do something else that made Dad to tell you about his job, you wouldn't tell me?"

She tightened her robe and narrowed her eyes. "What else would there be? Aren't I already dealing with enough?"

He stared at her flat stomach. "You don't *look* pregnant."

"It takes time, dipstick."

"Real mature. Are you gonna talk to your kid like that?"

"Shut up."

"Whatever." He opened the door. "If you see Dad, tell him I'm looking for him."

Zeke didn't wait for an answer before slamming the door.

His stomach growled, reminding him that he needed to eat. And with all the time lost trying to find out what was going on with Hadley, he'd have to scarf his food down quickly and get back to his game. This was seriously the worst weekend for the HardCorps event. He needed to keep his standing, especially if he was finally going to start a gaming channel.

But he also needed to find out what Hadley was hiding.

Chapter Fourteen

BRAD PULLED up to Kurt's house. Every muscle in his body ached as he took in the huge house. This was the last place he wanted to be, but he had no other choice. When his boss invited him over, he went. End of story.

Especially now, with so much going on. Kurt might need convincing that Brad could still do his job while dealing with all the family drama — not that his boss knew the half of it. Or maybe he just wanted to check in on how the house construction was coming along.

Brad relaxed at that thought. Maybe that was all this little meeting was. Kurt was anxious for Brad to get back to the knife shop, so it made sense. Although, for that update, why not just ask Gary? The contractor would know a lot more about what was going on than Brad.

Unless he knew about what Hadley had done to Nate. Then he would have genuine cause for concern. Especially if he thought Brad spilled his secret to a teenager. But why would he think that? It hadn't been Brad's idea. Faye was the one to insist. And because Brad had a moment of weakness, he'd agreed.

His phone buzzed. A text from his boss: *Come on in. No need to wait.*

Brad looked up at the house, and though he couldn't see the security camera, he waved. Then he got out of the car and headed up the walkway.

Kurt was already waiting for him with the door open. "Come on in."

Brad's stomach twisted but he forced a smile. He followed his boss to the same dining room he and Faye had eaten in the last time they were over. The house was so big, it had numerous dining rooms — one large enough to hold everyone from BlueBlade.

The same young girl he'd met before brought out a breakfast spread. She made Brad uncomfortable. She didn't seem as old as Hadley, yet she wore a too-short dress and bustled about while serving them.

Kurt piled his plate high with food and spoke about some rumors about next season's Seahawks player trades.

Brad nodded in agreement and struggled to keep the conversation going as he put a little food on his plate. Football was the last thing on his mind.

"Don't be shy. Take more food than that." Kurt gave a hearty laugh.

"Just not that hungry this morning."

"Long night?"

"You could say that."

"Was the construction crew there too late?"

Brad shook his head. "And about that, we really appreciate you sending them over. Faye is thrilled about her in-home salon."

Kurt beamed. "Wonderful. I can't wait to have you back at the shop. And I'm sure you'll be happy to get away from the house."

"I don't mind being there. We have a lot going on."

"How's your mom?"

"She isn't complaining, so it's hard to tell. I know she'd rather be doing everything herself, but it just isn't possible."

Kurt nodded and swallowed. "And after her staying with you for a while, what do you think of the dementia diagnosis? You said before you didn't buy it."

Brad hesitated. He still suspected someone to be behind his mom's odd behavior, but he didn't know who or how. "I still have my questions about that, but I don't doubt she needs to be with us — for now, at least. Given some time, I wouldn't be surprised to see her living on her own again."

"Good, good. You think she'll be okay with Faye there working?"

"I would think so." He nearly said something about Hadley being there too, but stopped himself. That was a rabbit hole he didn't want to approach. "My mother is resilient, so I think once she recovers, she'll be right back to her old life."

"Perfect. Have some more crepes." Kurt waved toward the platters of food. "So, you'll be able to come into the shop next week if the construction is done?"

Brad stuffed a bite of omelet in his mouth to give himself a few moments to think before swallowing. "It's going to take some time to get everything set up."

"Gary's crew can help with that. It can be done in no time."

"There's also the matter of Faye giving her notice at her current salon. She can't just up and quit. As a boss, I'm sure you understand."

"Everyone has a price. I'll find her boss's."

Brad's muscles tensed. If he had to go into work, it would be far harder to get to the bottom of the car wash, finding out who was behind his mom's original injury, and making sure the social worker stopped asking about Hadley.

"It'll do you a world of good to get back into your routine." Kurt gave him a reassuring smile, almost as though he could read Brad's thoughts.

"Sure. If you need me to do some actual work from home, I can do that. Just tell me what you need me to do."

"I need you in the office. That isn't a problem, is it?"

Brad forced a smile. "No. Of course not."

"Perfect. So glad we'll have you in this coming week."

"Great." That meant he would have to work twice as fast while he still had time off to find the answers he needed. Plus catch up on his sleep and get rid of the lingering headache.

"Have you tried the breakfast wine?" Kurt gestured toward Brad's empty glass. "It's sweeter than most dessert varieties. Try it. Tell me if you pick up a light blueberry hint. My father can't taste it, but I'm telling you it's there. You can be the tie breaker."

Brad poured some. "Is Ralf around? I haven't seen him in some time."

"He's upstairs." Kurt motioned toward the ceiling. "Mom is traveling with friends, so Dad thought he'd stay here for company."

"He didn't want to join us for breakfast?"

"He was up before the sun and ate after his workout."

"That's impressive."

"Or crazy. Take your pick." Kurt laughed.

"How does he like retirement?"

Kurt's brow cocked slightly. "Retirement? He'll be working 'til the day he dies — and he'll want to work longer."

"I haven't seen him around the knife shop in, what, a year?"

"You know how it is, working behind the scenes. He still likes to deal with people directly. In-person handshakes and all of that." Kurt's eyes lit up. "That reminds me. I have your next assignment. This one is a little personal. He wants you to handle it."

"Not Scott?"

"He still hasn't fully recovered from his car wreck. This one is all you."

"Right. Okay."

"You able to handle it with everything going on at home?"

"Yes. Like I told you, I can handle my assignments no problem. It's getting into the shop that's the tricky part."

"And Gary's crew is working to fix that as we speak." Kurt rose and pushed his chair back. "I'm going to grab that file for you before I forget. But first, try the wine."

Brad had forgotten about that. He picked up the glass and took a sip. Tried to hide a wince at the shock of how sweet it was.

"Detect any blueberry?"

He couldn't pinpoint any particular taste. "It's like drinking maple syrup mixed with a bag of sugar."

"But do you taste blueberry?"

Brad forced another sip. Tried to find a hint of any berry. Thought there was a little something. Maybe. "Yeah, it's there."

Kurt beamed. "I can't wait to tell Father he was wrong."

"It's subtle." Brad drank water to clear his palate. "Really subtle."

"But it's there. I'll be right back with the file."

Brad nodded, gulping down more water.

"If you need anything else, just let the girls know." Kurt disappeared through the kitchen.

A moment later, one of the servers arrived. This one looked only slightly older than Hadley. "Can I get you anything else, Mr. Morris?"

"No, thank you."

She glanced at his wine glass. "More to drink, sir?"

He shook his head. "I'm fine, really."

"I can't get you anything?" Her gaze darted around. She fidgeted like she was nervous.

Maybe Kurt would get upset with her if she didn't serve him something.

"Actually, are there more crepes?" Brad motioned toward the empty platter. "I could use another."

The girl smiled. "Yes. I'll be right back with those."

She grabbed the plate and disappeared into the kitchen.

Brad leaned back and relaxed, glad to have a moment to himself.

Footsteps sounded.

He expected to see the girl again, or perhaps Kurt returning with the file.

It was Ralf Bergmann. The mysterious top dog at BlueBlade. He showed up so irregularly that many of the employees had never seen him.

Brad had met with him countless times over the years, but not recently. His beard was now fully white, contrasting with his leathery tanned skin, and his head was completely bald, or possibly shaved. He looked like the kind of guy to get up at the crack of dawn to exercise.

The older man's gaze bore into Brad's. Though he had to be in his seventies, he still managed to strike fear into Brad.

"Ralf, it's good to see you again."

The man nodded, barely.

Brad stood. "I hear you have an assignment for me in particular."

"Yes." Ralf didn't budge, or even blink.

The man was nothing if not intimidating.

"I look forward to the challenge."

Ralf pursed his lips and crossed his arms.

Brad's pulse thrummed in his ears. "Do you want something to eat?"

Ralf's brows furrowed. "Don't mess it up. This is personal to me."

"May I ask how?"

"He's up from the ring of people who killed my daughter. I'm getting close."

Brad's skin prickled. "I thought her killer was behind bars."

"Someone is in prison for the crime. Not the one responsible."

"I won't let you down."

Ralf looked him over. "Good."

Then he left.

Brad's breath hitched. He stared at the empty space.

A moment later, Kurt appeared where his dad had been, a file in hand. "Everything okay?"

"Yeah. Just spoke with your dad."

"He filled you in?"

Brad sat. "He said this guy was involved in your sister's death."

"Yes." Kurt handed him the file.

"Why don't you handle it? Don't you want revenge for her?"

"Once we get to the head boss, I might."

"Might?"

"I don't want to talk about it." Kurt took his seat. "Did you tell him you picked up the blueberry flavor?"

"No. I forgot."

"Well, I'll have to tell him, then." He poured himself some wine and took a sip. "Gary will let me know when your wife's salon is set up and ready. Then I'll see you at the shop. In the meantime, if you have any questions about your target, don't hesitate to ask."

Brad took that as his cue to leave, and put on his jacket. "Thanks for breakfast. And sending the work crew to my house."

"Can't have my best assassin stuck at home." Kurt laughed.

Brad forced himself to laugh along with his boss. "Right."

He breathed a sigh of relief once he was finally in his car. The timing wasn't the greatest so far as hunting down a target — especially one so important to the Bergmanns — but somehow he would manage to get everything done. Maybe he could even get in a nap, if he could find his earplugs.

As he pulled up to the house, a group of neighbors caught his attention.

So did a streak of blue in a sweep of raven-black hair.

The social worker was back, questioning the neighbors. No doubt about Hadley.

Brad pulled into the driveway. And from his rearview he saw the neighbors all turning his way.

Chapter Fifteen

Brad lifted a blind and peeked outside. The neighbors were still gathered across the street, but the social worker wasn't speaking with them.

It didn't mean she wasn't out of his line of sight, talking with others.

Didn't she have anything else to do? It was a Sunday morning. Did the woman not sleep? Was this personal? Or was she just trying to prove herself at work to advance her career?

None of it mattered. He was sick of everyone pointing fingers at his family.

Even though this time, it was legitimate.

But he wouldn't let his daughter go down for an accident. If Nate hadn't been antagonizing her, she wouldn't have lashed out at him. And if Wes hadn't threatened her, she likely wouldn't have had a knife on her in the first place.

That whole family was crazy, and they'd done everything to themselves. Wes had killed his wife and tried to pin it on Brad. He'd threatened a teenage girl. Nate had threatened to use a secret against Hadley.

They were far from innocent. And given that the apple never fell far from the tree, Nate might have killed Hadley if she hadn't stood up for herself. If Nate's own dad had killed his mom, what would stop Nate from killing a girl from school who he thought was a threat?

Hadley had no other choice. Nate shouldn't have followed her.

Brad let go of the blind and stepped away from the window. He'd really wanted to try for a nap after returning home, but now his nerves were on edge. There was no way he could sit still, much less settle down enough to sleep.

It was just as well. He had too much to do anyway.

Especially now with the new target. This one would be different. Not only because it was so important to the Bergmanns, but because he'd been targeted himself when going out for his last two hits.

He would handle this one completely on his own. Nobody, not even Kurt or anyone else from BlueBlade, would know when he was leaving or where he was going. If they wanted to follow him, it would take a lot more work on their part.

And he had more reason than ever to suspect the people he was working for. Who exactly, he didn't know. Was it Kurt? Maybe. Someone else? Possibly. But the fact that Wes worked for the Slippery Fish and so had his dad — who had apparently also been an assassin, and was killed for it — was a red flag. Not to mention the fact that Rose, who'd been involved with Wes, had been gunning for Brad.

Now Kurt was making it harder for Brad to look into the car wash.

Fat chance.

Now he was more determined than ever.

Brad settled into his chair and did a basic online search about the Slippery Fish. He got the history easily enough — the public face. It had been around long enough to prove the dates in his dad's logbook to be true. There wasn't much else. No pictures or mentions of his dad. None of Wes, either.

Pound! Bang! Thump! Chink! Thud!

Brad turned on some music to drown out the construction noise. Narrowed his eyes to focus.

Thump! Chink! Thud!

Plugged his ears. Could still hear pounding and banging.

Looked around for his earplugs. Couldn't find them anywhere. Probably took them somewhere else.

Pound! Bang! Thump!

Were they working right outside his office?

Bang! Thump! Chink!

He got up, tempted to throw something from his desk across the room. Instead, he gathered his things and headed downstairs. Found Faye and let her know he was going to get some work done elsewhere.

"It's pretty loud, isn't it?"

"You could say that," he muttered.

"Do you know when you'll be back? Your mom is getting antsy."

"Take her and the kids to her house."

"What?" Faye cupped her ears.

Brad tried to push aside his annoyance and leaned closer to repeat himself.

She nodded. "At least it will be quiet there."

"Right. Since nobody will be home, will you lock our bedroom door?"

"What?"

"Never mind." He hurried upstairs and locked it himself, after grabbing a few more items to take to his mom's house later.

He checked on Zeke. Playing his video game, of course. He pulled off his son's headphones. "Your mom is taking everyone to your grandma's house."

Zeke scowled. "But I'm behind on my XP. Leaving will just make it worse!"

He clearly wasn't bothered by the noise.

"Take it up with your mom. If you get hungry, you're on your own."

"I don't care."

"Talk to your mom."

Zeke put his headphones back on and turned back to his game.

By the time Brad made it downstairs again, Faye was already helping his mom into her coat. Hadley and Luna were getting their shoes on.

"Can you get Zeke?" Faye asked.

"He wants to stay!" Brad made sure to say it loud enough.

"This racket isn't getting to him?"

"I don't think he can hear anything over his game!"

"He can stay!"

Outside, his ears rang. He could still hear the now muffled noise.

"Where are you going?" Faye asked.

"You aren't coming with us?" His mom frowned.

Brad shook his head. "I need to get some work done. That isn't going to happen here."

"You can work in Dad's office. I'm sure it'd have made him happy to have you in there."

He gave her a half-smile. "I bet it would have. Maybe I'll stop by in a while and do that. How are you feeling?"

She rubbed one of her stitches. "Been better, but can't complain."

"Take it easy over there." He helped her into Faye's car and said goodbye to everyone before going to his.

At least the street was empty. With any luck, the social worker was taking the rest of the day off. The last thing he needed was to worry about her, or what any of the neighbors were saying about his family.

Brad waited for Faye to drive off before starting his car. His headache was threatening to return. Hopefully getting away from the noise would help. Maybe he'd even pick up a coffee. Caffeine almost always helped.

Though at this point, it would be a miracle if anything worked. Just glancing back at his house made it worse.

He dug through his glove box to see if he had any ibuprofen left, but couldn't find any. Thought over his plan to get work done elsewhere. His eyes hurt too much to strain looking at a screen. The letters seemed to be getting smaller these days.

Maybe what he needed to do was watch the car wash. See who was coming and going. It might be a bad time — people would most likely stay home on a Sunday.

Or maybe they would be more likely to go because it *seemed* like the ideal time to stay away.

Yes. It was the perfect time for a stakeout. Kurt had told him to leave well enough alone, but that was the last thing Brad would do.

He couldn't take his car. Too many in the business would recognize it. Taking one of the company vehicles would give him the same problem.

His gaze landed on Hadley's car. It screamed teenage girl with the fuzzy steering wheel, purple license plate frames, and heart decals in the corners of the windows.

It was perfect.

Brad cut his engine, gathered his things again, and put them in her car. He slid on a baseball cap and sunglasses before remote-locking his car and texting Hadley so she wouldn't freak if she came home and saw her car missing.

She wasn't happy, but she'd get over it. And she'd be getting over it in the comfort of her own room instead of a jail cell.

As soon as he started the engine, loud music blared from the speakers. He turned down the volume and headed for town. Drove around the block so he could check out the car wash, but he didn't recognize anyone. Didn't recognize any of the vehicles, either. He pulled into the parking lot, choosing a spot in front of one of the stores at the strip mall that shared the lot with the Slippery Fish.

He could almost see inside the building. The way it was set up, the cars went through the middle of the structure for the cleaning. On either side of the wash were windows that allowed those inside to peek in at various stages. Luna would probably love sitting in the waiting room, watching the cars go through.

People came and went. Apparently, Sunday was a popular day for cleaning cars.

Brad stayed low, keeping an eye out for anyone he recognized. If he saw someone from BlueBlade, he would consider that jackpot. Considering Rose had been involved with Wes, she couldn't be the only one with ties to the other assassin ring. There had to be others.

What he needed to know was if the Bergmanns were connected to this place. If so, they would be involved at the top.

It was hard to see exactly who was coming and going. His best bet might be to go through the car wash. He would hardly be able to stay hidden that way, but at least he would be in a vehicle nobody would expect him to drive. And he did have the hat and sunglasses.

It might be enough.

But if someone did recognize him, he would be in the middle of the car wash. Anyone inside could see him.

His pulse raced at the thought. It wasn't the best position to put himself in. But he could act like he was just washing his daughter's car. What was suspicious about that? Even Kurt couldn't get irritated with him for disobeying direct orders. He was just washing his pregnant — sick — daughter's car.

Or he could try to up his disguise. Hadley might have one of her wigs from her various plays in the car. He could throw on some lipstick to finish the look.

No. That was going too far. He'd go with the innocent washing of his child's car. He could argue the specifics with Kurt if it came down to it. Where else in town was he supposed to go? It was too cold to wash it in the driveway.

Yes. That would be the plan.

With any luck, nobody would recognize him and stop the car wash halfway through.

But if they did, at least he would know the truth.

Chapter Sixteen

BRAD LOOKED around the car for anything else he could add to his disguise — just in case he needed something quickly. But he only saw makeup and stray clothes. Nothing useful.

It was just as well.

He restarted the engine and headed for the car wash, checking to make sure he had enough cash. It was a habit to keep plenty on hand for times like this when he didn't want to leave a record of being somewhere. But sometimes the stash dwindled before he could restock.

Luckily, he had a few twenties. That would be more than enough.

He got in line behind a muddy SUV, then slid one of the twenties into the machine upon reaching it. Got a receipt that he would later destroy, stuffed it in his pocket, and waited.

There were three lights above the entrance that looked a traffic signal. Currently, the red one was lit.

It turned green.

Brad readjusted his baseball cap and sunglasses before

easing off the brake. The car was an automatic, and it inched toward the entrance.

Not even a minute later, the track was pulling the vehicle inside. He felt like a kid again, his heart thumping extra hard heading into a car wash, but this was for entirely different reasons. He might see one of his coworkers inside.

If he did, then he would have a whole new path to follow. He'd be that much closer to finding out the truth. Because one thing was for sure — he wasn't going back to the county jail to visit Rose or Wes. His chat with Rose, while not entirely useless, hadn't been the success he'd hoped for. And he doubted Wes would even speak with him.

He patted his pocket where he kept his gun and stared straight ahead as he came up to the windows. Threw in a fake yawn for good measure as he glanced at the people in the waiting room out of the corners of his eyes. Considering how many cars were going through, there were surprisingly few people inside.

And none of them were BlueBlade employees. He didn't recognize a single person.

He might have to wash all three of the family cars. Plus his mom's. And even then, he might not find anything — the odds that he'd go through at exactly the right time to catch someone from BlueBlade were minimal.

Getting to the bottom of this could take some real creativity. It would be especially challenging if he went back to work on top of taking care of his family's needs.

He would make it happen. It wasn't like he expected any of this to be easy. Nothing had been so far.

Brad kept his focus on the people inside, burning their images into his memory. One of them might come into BlueBlade, and he needed to recognize them when they did. He had to see who they spoke to, and maybe more importantly, who they *didn't* but made lingering eye contact with in passing.

Maybe going back to work was exactly what he needed now. He'd have to be sure to thank Kurt again for setting up the annoying construction on his house.

Brad started to relax as he came up near the end of the car wash. He was slightly disappointed he hadn't seen anyone he knew, but the answers would come. Every moment, he was getting closer to finding out who killed his dad.

Just before the strips of cloth lowered to dry the car, someone inside caught Brad's attention.

A man in a white tennis outfit with tanned leathery skin, a white beard, and a bald head.

Ralf Bergmann.

The head of BlueBlade was at the Slippery Fish. Brad had just seen him at breakfast, so there was no doubt. It was definitely him.

He forced himself not to stare. Not that anyone would notice with the mass of cloth drying Hadley's car all around him.

Ralf was speaking with a guy around Brad's age near the employee area.

Brad craned his neck for a better view. Not that it helped.

As soon as the rack of cloths lifted, the track pulled the car forward. He was surrounded by brick walls on either side and the bright daylight in front of him.

Brad looked back, trying to see inside, but it was too late. A van was now approaching, blocking any view he might've otherwise had.

He drove around the other side of the building, vying for another peek. It was impossible to see where Ralf had been because there were no windows. He inched forward, rounding the entire structure, still unable to see anything useful.

There had to be something he could do. Couldn't go inside.

A Bentley. Parked in a spot by itself marked *Reserved.*

Interesting. Who else would bring such an expensive car here? Surely, Ralf Bergmann had people to hand wash his Bentley with pricy imported soap and a diaper.

He was here on business. No doubt about that.

Brad squeezed the steering wheel and parked in a spot where he could watch both the Bentley and the building. His mind raced. Should he confront Ralf? Follow him? Act casual, as if surprised to see him?

There was no doubt he would mention the run-in to his son, and Kurt had already warned Brad to drop his suspicions about the Slippery Fish.

He would be better off taking this slowly. See where Ralf went after this. Look for the ideal spot to bump into the man.

Time dragged on. Ralf hadn't returned to his car after twenty minutes.

Brad's phone rang.

He reached for it, partially expecting it to be one of the Bergmanns saying they knew what he was doing, and he was going to be disciplined.

It was Faye.

He accepted the call, staring at the car wash. "How's it going?"

"It's a lot quieter here. Your mom wants to cook for us. Do you mind picking up a few things from the store?"

Fantastic timing. "Sure. What does she need?"

"I'll text you a list."

A list. Even better. "I'll get on that shortly. I'm finishing up some work."

"Can't they ever give you a break?"

"I have extra on my plate, given current circumstances. How's Hadley holding up?"

Faye sighed on the other end. "She's really worried about someone finding out."

"Tell her I have that handled. In fact, I'm working on that as we speak."

"You are?"

"Yes. I'm—"

A side door of the building opened.

Brad stared, unblinking.

"Are you there?" Faye said. "Did we get cut off?"

"I'll fill you in when I get there. Text me the list. Love you." He ended the call and shoved the phone in his pocket.

Ralf stepped outside and looked around.

Brad lowered himself in the seat, watching the older man between the dashboard and the top of the steering wheel.

Ralf waved to someone inside before closing the door behind him. Walked straight for the Bentley. Passed Brad.

His breath hitched.

Ralf kept looking straight ahead. Remote unlocked his car and got in.

Brad put his hands on the key to start his engine. Waited for the Bentley to pull out and followed it, keeping a good distance between the two cars.

Ralf was heading toward the freeway.

That left Brad with two choices — continue following him or let him go. He'd promised Faye the list of groceries, but now he had proof that the head of his assassination ring was involved with the other operation in town. Once

Ralf got on the freeway, he could go anywhere. He could be on the road for hours.

It wouldn't be fair to Faye, who was taking care of *his* mother and Hadley. He'd been gone most of the morning since he'd accepted Kurt's invitation to breakfast. But at the same time, when would he get an opportunity like this again?

Ralf turned into a parking lot just before the onramp, saving Brad the decision.

Brad slowed before turning in. It was a small lot with few cars. Hardly the ideal place for spying, especially in a car as easy to identify as Hadley's. It had a small run-down building off to the side. Pine trees surrounded the edge, giving the place privacy.

He parked beside a boat of a car that hid him, positioning himself so he could still kind of see through the windows to watch Ralf. His only option, unless he wanted to risk being seen. He cut the engine and waited. Couldn't see the boss getting out of his vehicle.

His phone buzzed with a text. Faye clearly wanted to know where he was. He didn't need to look at the screen to know what was happening. He'd get back to her later.

Brad kept waiting for Ralf. Ten minutes became twenty, then thirty. His phone buzzed again. He wasn't going to take his attention off the Bentley to look.

It buzzed again.

What if it was an emergency? Something could've gone wrong with either his mom or daughter. Or they could've found proof of something in the house. Brad was sure someone was messing with her medications, and that was why she took her initial fall.

He reached for his phone, but couldn't grab it without looking away from Ralf.

The messages were from Faye, but it didn't sound like

anyone was injured. She kept asking where he was. He replied that he was still working on Hadley's thing, and that he'd get the groceries ASAP. Then he put the phone on the dashboard where he could see the screen when she texted again.

Tap, tap.

Brad nearly jumped out of his skin. Turned to see Ralf standing at his door.

He swore, took off his hat and sunglasses, then got out of the car. "What are you doing here?"

Ralf's forehead wrinkled. "I came to ask you the same thing."

"What were you doing at the car wash?"

"I don't believe I'm required to answer to you," Ralf said.

"They're covering another assassin ring. But you obviously already know that, or you wouldn't have been there."

"What makes you think that?"

No way Brad was going to show all of his cards. "It's where Wes Campbell worked."

Ralf nodded, staring Brad down.

"There's no denying Wes was involved in the other ring."

"Didn't my son already tell you to drop this?"

Brad clenched his jaw. "It all hits too close to home for me to just forget about it. I need answers."

"I'm going to tell you this once." Ralf's brows furrowed. "Then you need forget about this. As in, don't repeat it and don't think about it."

Brad didn't budge.

"Understood?"

"How are the two companies connected?"

Ralf's eyes narrowed and he stepped closer, his nostrils flaring. "I said, understood?"

Brad's pulse quickened. For a man in his seventies, Ralf was every bit as intimidating as his younger counterparts. "Yes."

"Good." His boss took a single step back. "Yes, the two companies are indeed connected — but not in the way you think."

"What does that mean?"

"It means you drop it before something you don't want happens to you."

"What's going to happen to me?"

"Nothing, because you're going to drop all of this and forget any of it ever happened."

Forget Wes and Rose worked together to frame him for murder? Forget his dad was murdered by someone in the other assassin ring? Not a chance.

"Don't forget what happened to Felix." Ralf spun around and returned to his car.

And there it was: a threat to kill Brad and make an example out of him.

Chapter Seventeen

Zeke yanked off his headphones, too famished to ignore the hunger any longer, then went downstairs to find some food.

Everything was especially quiet. Maybe the construction crew was taking a lunch. The silence was nice and made choosing what to eat easier. As soon as he sat to take the first bite of another microwaved burrito, his mind wandered back to his dad.

An assassin. It could actually be kind of cool, but he was too freaked out to feel that way. His dad killed people. Had been lying to them for years. And he'd been drilling the importance of honesty into Zeke's head all that time.

Hypocrite.

If only Hadley was home. They'd probably told her more than they'd told him. Who knew what else Dad had done?

Their dad — Mr. Perfect — wasn't so perfect after all. The man was a killer.

It seemed like a bad dream. Except it was real.

The key sounded in the lock, and as the door opened, he heard his mom, sisters, and grandma talking.

Mom appeared in the doorway. "You haven't seen your dad, have you?"

He swallowed a bite of burrito and shook his head no.

She frowned. "Of course not. Do you know what time the crew left?"

"Nope. Just got down here. Why? What's up?"

"Nothing." She looked at his plate with one bite left. "What are you eating?"

"Frozen burrito."

Mom sighed. "I need to warm up something for the rest of us. Dad was supposed to pick up some food and bring it to us over there, but something more important came up." She flung open the fridge and then the freezer, slamming things around.

"Let's order pizza. I'm still hungry."

She shook her head. "We're not doing takeout right now."

"Fine. Want me to warm something up?"

Mom looked at him like he'd grown a third eye. "Just finish your burrito. I'll figure something out."

"You sure?"

She glared at him with a death stare.

Zeke scrambled from the chair and hurried upstairs. He was just trying to help, and she was getting mad at him for it. He'd wait to finish eating.

Hadley stepped out of the bathroom when he reached the landing. She started for her room.

"Wait," he called, racing over.

She turned. "What do you want?"

"Have you thought more about Dad being an assassin?"

"What about it?"

"Are you kidding me? He kills people for a living. *Our dad.*"

She shrugged.

Had he stepped into an alternate universe? Zeke took a step closer. "Listen to yourself. Our dad is a *killer.*"

"Didn't we already have this conversation?"

"What is wrong with you? He's a total hypocrite! Expecting honesty from us when he's been lying this whole time. Telling us not to hit anyone when he does so much worse."

Hadley sighed dramatically. "He never had to tell *me* not to strike anyone."

Anger rushed through Zeke like a raging river. "You don't even care?"

"I have bigger problems."

"Yeah, you're pregnant and your twenty-five-year-old boyfriend is dead. I get it. But our dad is an *assassin*! A killer. You really can't top that."

"Shut up!" Spittle flew from her mouth and her face reddened. "I hate you!"

She stormed into her room and slammed the door shut.

Zeke stared in disbelief. What just happened?

He didn't care. It had been a stupid idea to try talking to her in the first place. She didn't care about anything but herself. And her stupid baby.

His stomach rumbled for more food. No way was he going downstairs. His mom was in just as bad a mood as Hadley. Unfortunately, he was surrounded by females, and he wasn't taking any chances with the other two. He was better off in his own room with his game, even if his stomach was screaming at him.

The aroma of either lasagne or spaghetti wafted up from the living room, making his mouth water. He'd wait until everyone else was done eating. It wasn't worth dealing with the crazy.

Zeke emptied his backpack on his bed and looked through his homework. He didn't want to think about any of it, but it was Sunday and the hours were flying by.

Knock, knock.

"I'm not hungry!"

The knob twisted.

He rolled his eyes and waited for his mom to appear in the doorway.

It was Hadley.

"What do you want? To tell me again how much you hate me?"

She took a deep breath. "Look, I didn't mean that. I'm under a *lot* of stress. Like seriously, you have no idea."

"Okay."

"Can I use your phone? Please?" She gave him her puppy-dog eyes that always worked on Dad.

Zeke wasn't Dad. "What's wrong with yours?"

"I don't have it."

"Why not?"

"Mom and Dad have it."

"Why'd they take it?"

Hadley put her hands on her hips. "Does it matter?"

"There must be a reason they don't want you making calls."

"And suddenly you're Mr. High and Mighty?"

"Who do you need to call?"

"Nobody. I just have to check social media."

"What about your laptop or tablet?"

"They have those, too."

"Geez. What'd you do?"

She held up her hand like she was going to slap him.

"For real, Hadley?"

Her hand dropped. "Mom is losing her mind. She thinks I'm going to do something crazy. I'm *not*. I just need to know what people are saying about Nate."

"You just want to know if he's been found?" It had never occurred to him that his sister might actually be worried about someone else — someone who had nothing to do with her own problems.

She nodded.

Zeke pulled out his phone. "I'll look."

"I need to check *my* accounts. See what my friends are saying."

"My friends are probably saying the same thing."

"All they're probably posting is screenshots of HardCorps."

He put away his phone.

"Okay, okay. See what they're saying."

"Why? My friends are just a bunch of video gaming nerds, right?"

"Let me see."

Zeke shook his head. "I have homework to do."

"Come *on*. I need to know what people are saying."

"Even my dumb friends?"

"I didn't say that."

"You may as well have."

"Either let me look, or you look. I don't care which. All that matters is finding out what people are saying."

"Why is it so important?"

"He's your friend, too! Don't you care?"

Zeke took a deep breath. "Yes, but I'm pretty sure he just ran away. Can't say I'd blame him. His dad is in jail for killing his mom, and now his aunt is going to move them away."

Relief covered her face. "You really think that? Is that what most people think?"

"Why wouldn't they?"

"Then let me see your phone. Or your tablet. I don't care which one. Please. I have to see what people are saying."

"Fine. You better give it back."

"I will."

He unlocked his phone, opened a social media app, and tossed it, ready to chase her if she ran off with it. Pregnant or not, he'd tackle Hadley if she tried to steal it.

But she didn't budge. Just scrolled up and down the screen. At one point she looked up at him and said, "Boys are so gross."

"Your point?" He didn't even care what she was referring to. "Anything about Nate?"

"Not really. Most of it's about your stupid game."

"It isn't stupid," he snapped.

Hadley kept scrolling. "Mind if I log you out and check my account?"

"Well, since you're being so nice to me …"

She glared at him.

"Why don't you just ask for your stuff back?"

"I told you — Mom's going crazy."

"Then ask Dad."

"Whose side you think he'll take?"

Zeke shrugged.

"So, can I check my account or not?"

He drew a deep breath. "I can't remember my password. Use the incognito browser on my laptop."

"Good idea." She leaped for his desk.

"Did you just say I had a good idea?"

"Don't get a big head. I need you to unlock your screensaver."

"Then move." He sat and typed his password before opening an anonymous screen.

Her fingers flew across the keyboard, and a few seconds later, she was scrolling through her social media feed.

Zeke peeked over her shoulder. Mostly pictures of high school couples on dates. It was like they all were all competing to prove they'd had the best time. Probably their version of bragging about leveling up and earning better items in the game.

"Find anything?"

"Nobody's talking about him that I can see. I'm going to need to do a search."

"Have fun." He didn't budge, watching her type Nate's name into the bar.

A bunch of results popped up, mostly posts he'd made before disappearing. Hadley clicked on his profile. Nothing from him since the morning he was last seen. She scrolled down, as if that would tell them anything.

"Some people are commenting on his stuff, asking where he is."

"Maybe you should, too."

She whipped around, her eyes wide. "Why do you think that?"

"I thought you two weren't getting along. It might make him feel better. But whatever."

Hadley frowned. "That's probably a good idea. It'll look like I care — which I do."

"Never said you didn't."

She started typing, and he inched closer to read what people were saying.

"Does this sound okay?" she asked.

He leaned closer for a look.

Hey, Nate. Hope everything's OK. Check in soon. I'm starting to get worried. ~H

"Sounds fine to me."

"Maybe I should have Dad read it over."

"Dad?" Zeke exclaimed. "What's gotten into you? Since when do you want his approval for anything?"

"I don't want his *approval*. Just his opinion. What's wrong with that?"

"Nothing, but I'd just post it. There's nothing bad about it. Pretty generic, if you ask me."

"Too generic?"

He studied her. She was definitely acting weird. But he had homework to do, if he wanted to get back on the game tonight. "It's great. I'm sure he'll like it when he sees it. Can I have my computer back now?"

Hadley turned back to the screen. "I thought you were doing homework. Let me look around some more."

He sighed and looked at the stuff on his bed. "Just don't go snooping. Stay on that incognito tab."

"Trust me, I don't want to see whatever you're trying to hide."

"Good." He scowled at the back of her head before going through his books, trying to figure out which subject he wanted to avoid the least. It was all pointless.

He pulled an English worksheet from his notebook and got to work. It didn't take long for his mind to wander to his YouTube channel. Now that he had the money, he needed to get going with his plan. Time was of the essence, but nobody would drive him to the store.

Then a thought struck him. "Will you drive me to Wilson's?"

"Why?"

He bit back a sarcastic comment. "Because I'm letting you use my computer when Mom and Dad said no."

She turned around and frowned. "I couldn't even if I wanted."

"Why not? Lose your license?"

"Shut up. Dad took my car."

"Why?"

"Got me. He texted me but he didn't explain. I guess he thinks everything belongs to him."

"Sounds about right." Zeke got back to his sheet, then to math next.

Homework was so boring and pointless. When would he ever need any of this in real life? Sure, he used basic math playing his game, but that was about it. He didn't need to figure out the value of x, y, or z, or know the proper usage of predicates. Chat speak was all he really needed. It wasn't like his future channel followers would care about his dangling participles. So lame.

He finished his math, then got up and stretched. He was antsy to move around. "How much longer are you going to be?"

"I'm still searching. People *are* talking about him. And me — they're still hung up on me and Duke."

"Wait 'til they find out about your pregnancy."

She gave him the death glare.

"Just sayin'." He looked outside. "If you're gonna be much longer, I'm going to ask if I can play HardCorps at Wynn's."

"Sounds good."

"That was your cue to give back my computer."

She continued typing. "It isn't like I have anything I can use."

"Fine. Don't go snooping — on the desktop or anything in my room. I'll know."

"Like I said, I don't *want* to see anything you're hiding. Don't feel like being grossed out."

"And you will be." He grabbed his phone and texted Wynn. "I'll be back."

Mom was in the hall. "There's food downstairs. I know this is a long shot, but do you know where Hadley is?"

"In my room. I'm going to Wynn's."

She lifted a brow. "Hadley's in there?"

"Yeah." He rushed to the stairs.

"Why?"

"She just is." He darted down to the kitchen, suddenly remembering the depth of his hunger. Scarfed down some lasagna while texting his friend.

Once outside, he noticed Dad's car was still there but Hadley's was gone.

Everyone was acting strange. It would be a relief to be around Wynn.

A block away, someone called his name.

The social worker.

"I don't have time to talk!"

She jogged over, though it appeared awkward in heels. "I just have a few questions."

"Look, I don't know anything about Nate. If I hear anything, I'll tell you. Okay?"

"Do you know where your sister was the night he disappeared?"

"She's always at home these days. Hasn't even been going to school."

"Why not?"

He suddenly felt defensive of his sister. Wasn't going to tell this nosy busybody about the pregnancy. "Health issues."

"Really?" She tilted her head. "Like what?"

"I have to go." Zeke bolted away before the social worker could say anything else.

Chapter Eighteen

BRAD STARED AT THE HOUSE, not wanting to get out of the car. He was exhausted from his interaction with Ralf.

There were too many questions — and he'd wanted to solve his father's murder since he was sixteen. He was close, and the last thing he would do was stop looking into it.

But first, he owed it to Faye to help out however he could.

Brad grabbed the grocery bags and headed inside. Surprisingly, it was quiet enough for him to hear Luna's cartoons playing in the living room. The house smelled of cooked food. Something Italian.

His stomach knotted. He was too late with the groceries — his mom would be disappointed and Faye would be mad.

At least he could explain himself to his wife. He didn't want to get his mom's hopes up about solving the murder until he knew he was close to proving something. Maybe not until there was an arrest. She was going through enough, and if her mind was as fragile as her body, he didn't want to risk upsetting her.

He put the groceries away, then found his mom in the living room with Luna. They were playing a board game while a show about unicorn princesses played in the background.

Brad put his arm around his mom. "Sorry I'm so late getting back with the food."

"I know you're busy." She gave him a reassuring smile. "But you did get them?"

"Just got done putting them away."

"Since we already had lunch, I'll cook dinner."

He glanced at her arm in a cast and sling, and one foot with a boot. "Sure you're up for it?"

She scratched a stitch on her face. "I may not be allowed near stairs, but I can handle making a meal."

"Let us know if you need any help." He kissed Luna hello before heading upstairs. Faye wouldn't be nearly so happy to see him. But she would understand his need to find answers, not only about his dad's murder, but also about Allison's.

Faye was in Zeke's room with Hadley, who sat at the desk. Their son was nowhere to be seen.

"I brought the groceries. Mom said she wants to make dinner. Why are you guys here?"

Hadley whipped around. "I want my electronics back."

"That doesn't explain why we're all congregated in Zeke's room."

"Because I can't get online any other way." Her eyes narrowed.

"And your brother let you use his?"

"Yep. He trusts me."

Brad stepped closer. "You know why we had to take your phone."

"Had to." She snorted. "And also my tablet and laptop. I can't even do homework!"

"Is that what you're doing now?"

Faye jumped in. "She's reading what kids are saying about Nate."

Brad's heart skipped a beat, and he put his hand on his daughter's shoulder. "You haven't confessed, have you?"

"No, and I'm not going to. I swear."

"Why'd you say it, then?"

"I was scared. But I realize it would be dumb. Why turn myself in when you got rid of all the evidence? You know what you're doing."

"It's a big risk, honey. I have to be fully sure you won't say anything that could implicate yourself. The last thing any of us want is for you to spend the rest of your life in prison. Do you know what it's like there?"

Her brows furrowed. "Do you?"

"I know enough."

"Trust me, Dad. That's the last place I want to go. I have this baby to think about."

His knees wobbled. "You aren't thinking of keeping it, are you?"

"I don't know what I'm going to do, aside from giving it a chance at life. This baby is Duke's. Part of him will live on through him or her, whether I adopt it out or keep it."

"You don't want to do that."

"I don't know what I want."

Faye put her hand on Hadley's. "Have you thought about telling his family? Maybe one of them would want to adopt. They might see it as a blessing, in light of the tragic loss."

Hadley pressed her palms on her stomach. "I see it that way, too. And because of that, I don't know what I want to do. It wouldn't be fair to get their hopes up, so I'm not going to say anything for now."

"You have time to decide," Faye reassured her.

"Can I get my stuff back?" Hadley glanced up at Brad. "Zeke's room smells funky."

He sniffed the air. He didn't smell anything unusual. "How can we be sure you won't tell anyone what happened?"

She rubbed her belly dramatically. "Because I don't want anything happening to this. Someone could punch me in the gut in prison. No way I'm going to risk that."

Brad exchanged a look with Faye. "Your mom and I will discuss it, then get back to you."

Her eyes lit up. "Really?"

"Yes. Sit tight while we talk."

"Thank you!" Hadley leaped up and wrapped her arms around him, squeezing tight, before also embracing Faye. Then she returned to the computer, typing frantically on her brother's keyboard.

Brad took Faye's hand and led her to their bedroom, locking the door behind them.

She pulled away. "What's going on with you?"

"What? I thought we were here to discuss Hadley."

"I think we should return her devices. Now, where were you all day?"

"First, I went to Kurt's for breakfast."

"Yes. But after that?"

"I went to the Slippery Fish."

Faye lifted a brow. "You were at a car wash all this time?"

"Wes worked there, and he was involved with Rose — both of them have framed me for murder. My *dad* worked at the car wash part-time. Did I show you the log book?"

She leaned against the dresser and drew a deep breath.

"I thought we agreed you'd wait to look into your dad's murder until we have less on our plates? I want to find his killer, too, but this isn't the time."

"But BlueBlade is involved."

"With your dad's murder?"

Brad wrung his hands together. "Yes. Ralf was at the car wash. Ralf!"

"He was probably getting his car cleaned."

"Nobody puts a Bentley through one of those."

"Our daughter is pregnant and accidentally killed her friend, your mom needs a lot from us right now, and our house is under construction. There isn't time to deal with more."

"I can do it all."

"Really?" She crossed her arms. "Is that why you were here all day helping me with your mom and our daughter?"

"I brought home groceries, and Mom said she'd make dinner. I'll help her with that. And more importantly, I now have proof of a link between the car wash and the knife shop."

"Great. Now can we focus on what's in front of us? I can't keep doing this alone. You need to step up and help me."

Silence hung between them as they stared each other down.

"Can you do that?" she asked.

"Yes, I promise to help more. I'll be here all day while you're at work."

"Are you going to be present? Not just here physically?"

"Of course."

"And what about Hadley?"

"We're going to return her devices."

Faye shook her head. "I mean, is she going back to

school? She seems to be feeling better, and we can't keep her home forever."

"Sure we can."

"Are you going to homeschool her? Because I don't have time for that."

"We can look into online school. Nobody'll have to know about the pregnancy. It'll also keep her from getting questioned about Nate."

"We've already coached her on how to handle that. And don't you think it'll look suspicious if she quits school right after his disappearance?"

"She wouldn't be quitting — she'd be doing homeschool or online school."

"But with people saying she and Nate were arguing before he disappeared, I don't think that's a good idea. Hadley needs to go to school, act like everything is normal, and let this fizzle out."

"A murder investigation isn't going to fizzle out."

"He's a missing person who has been through hell recently. People might think he's searching for his biological parents, since he'll never see his adopted parents again."

Brad rubbed his temples. "Okay, say we send her back to school. What about her stomach? It's going to get bigger."

"If she's anything like me, she won't show in the first trimester and she'll be able to easily hide it in the second. By the time we have to worry about any of that, she'll be on summer break."

"Okay, we'll give it a try. But if things start to go south, we're pulling her. No questions asked."

Faye hesitated before answering. "Agreed."

"Are you going to break it to her that she needs to return tomorrow?"

"Sure. But she might want another day to rest and catch up on her homework. I think we should give that to her."

He was about to complain about juggling the construction, his mom, and Hadley, but then stopped himself, considering Faye had done exactly that all day today. "Sounds like a plan."

"Great. I'll tell her." She headed for the door, then stopped and looked at him. "You'll leave the car wash stuff alone for now? I'm not saying forever, just for now until things calm down."

"I won't let it interfere with our family again."

She tilted her head.

"It won't happen again. I give you my word."

"There's so much else going on."

"And I'm aware of all that. I'll prioritize my responsibilities better from here on out. Lesson learned." He wrapped his arms around her and gave her a kiss. "No more repeats of today."

"Okay, thanks." But she was frowning.

He knew he should address it, but didn't want to start another argument. "I should check on my mom. She might be ready to start on dinner."

"And I'd better break the news to Hadley."

They stepped into the hallway just in time to hear banging downstairs.

Brad turned to her. "Does Gary have a key?"

"To the new salon entrance."

"Perfect. Do you know when they're going to be done?"

She shook her head. "He said they're supposed to finish as quickly as possible."

"I can't wait."

"Be sure to thank Kurt again. I'm excited to give notice

tomorrow. Then on my lunch break, I'm going to start working on my website."

"Do you have a name for the business yet? What about getting licensed, or whatever you have to do?"

"I obviously already have my stylist license. Kurt said he's going to take care of the business license. I'll be all set soon." She beamed.

Kurt must really want to shut him up. He kept that thought to himself and gave her a kiss. "I'm really happy for you. I know how long you've wanted this."

He headed downstairs, finding his mom already in the kitchen. "Did I get everything you need?"

She smiled at him. "Yes. Thanks, sweetheart. Why don't you kick your feet up and rest? I know you've been busy all day."

"I'm more concerned about you. Do you need help?"

"Nah. I've got this."

Brad started to object when the doorbell rang. He opened it without looking outside, assuming it was Gary or one of the crew.

It was a decision he immediately regretted.

The social worker stood at the door. "Hello, Mr. Morris."

"What do you want?"

"I'd like to ask a few more questions about Nate."

He didn't open the door any wider than it already was. "We have nothing more to say. All of us hope he's found soon. Do you have any new leads?"

She eyed him with suspicion. "Your kids' names keep coming up. Hadley's in particular."

His pulse raced, but he didn't let his worry show on his face. "We all know they were friends. Not great friends, but friends."

"What do you mean by 'not great friends'?"

He sighed. "They don't run in the same circles, but they hang out on occasion due to being neighbors. Their mothers were good friends."

"Do you mind if I speak with Hadley?"

"Actually, I do. She's in the middle of homework, and I want her to focus."

The lines between Jacinta's eyebrows deepened.

"Perhaps another time?"

"Oh, I'll be back. You can trust me on that."

"I'm sure I can." He closed the door between them, his heart racing.

That social worker was more aggressive than Detective Stewart had been with either of the murder investigations.

Did she have more motivation than she was letting on? Or could she possibly know what Hadley had done?

Chapter Nineteen

BRAD CHECKED on Hadley and his mom, who were doing homework and a crossword puzzle respectively in the living room, despite the cacophony of construction. He hated leaving them at home while he went out, but it would be far easier to get his errands done without them — not to mention the fact that he could swing by the Slippery Fish without anyone knowing. Besides, Hadley was feeling much better and could easily take care of her grandma for a spell. And the crew was there if anything got hairy for some reason, not that he expected it would.

He reminded them that he was going out, then went outside, checking the salon's progress. It was coming along shockingly fast. Two of the guys were already painting walls while others were installing sinks.

Faye could open her business that week. And Kurt would expect Brad back at the shop. Which was exactly why he needed to get to the bottom of the car wash while he still could.

He snapped a picture of the progress and texted it to Faye as he started the engine. Looked around for a hat, but didn't find anything. Not that it mattered. He was driving his own car. If anyone who knew him saw it, they'd know it was him staking out the Slippery Fish. No point in going incognito now that Ralf had caught him.

As he left the neighborhood, he debated whether to go to the hospital or the car wash first. He needed to pick up some meds for his mom and also get the result of Hadley's test. His stomach lurched at the thought of her having picked up any diseases.

If the news was bad, he wanted to wait. He needed to be at the top of his game when he checked out the Slippery Fish. And it wasn't like knowing the result a few minutes earlier would change anything. If something was wrong with Hadley, he'd drop everything to take care of it. His dad had been dead and his murderer walking free for decades. What was a little longer?

The parking lot was practically empty and nobody was in line. Brad drove around the building, only seeing a couple kids behind the counter. Nobody else. He nearly took his car through, but doubted he'd see much more from inside, given the few vehicles in the lot. Certainly no Bentleys.

Brad thought about leaving, but instead, he parked the car and marched inside, not caring that he would certainly get caught on camera. It was tempting to wave to Kurt and Ralf, or whoever ran this joint. But he kept his eyes straight ahead and went to the counter.

One of the bored-looking kids, barely old enough to grow a scraggly beard, said hi. "Getting a wash?"

Brad leaned against the counter. "What's it like working here?"

"Huh?"

"Pretty dull during the week?"

The kid shrugged. "Yeah, I guess."

"Looking for a job?" asked the other. He was tall and lanky with a prominent Adams apple. "Cuz we're already full."

"Who's your boss?" Brad studied a wall with a line of photos of the employees of the month. Neither of these two were pictured.

"Jasper," said the tall one.

So, it wasn't Ralf. Or at least not that these two knew. Then again, it wasn't like the regular employees at Blue-Blade knew about him, either.

These two were obviously not assassins.

Brad laughed at the thought.

"What's so funny?" asked Fuzzy. "You know Jasper?"

"No." Brad cleared his throat. "How long you two been working here?"

"Few months."

Not long at all.

"Does Jasper have a last name?"

They both shrugged.

"How often do you see him?"

"He comes by every day. Why?"

"Just curious."

"Look, man. Are you getting a car wash or not?"

Brad took a deep breath and looked around for clues, trying to buy a little more time. "Anyone else work here?"

"Lots of people. None of them are here now. Nobody washes their car on Mondays."

Figured.

"Did you know Wes Campbell?"

The two kids exchanged nervous looks.

Brad took that as a yes. "What about Rose Flores?"

They eyed each other again.

Not that it was surprising. Brad stepped away from the counter. "Thanks, boys. You've been very helpful."

"How?" one asked.

Brad responded with a wave as he left. He mentally went over their answers as he made his way back to his car. Some random guy name Jasper ran the place, and they knew both Wes and Rose. This place was definitely connected to BlueBlade.

Not that Ralf had tried to deny it. But what did he mean when he said they weren't connected like Brad thought? Was it an unfriendly alliance? Were they only working together to clean up a mess, but actually hated each other? Whatever it was, had to be important since Ralf had brought up the Felix incident.

Little did he know that wasn't going to silence Brad. Although, he was likely to find out soon enough, once he got word that Brad had questioned those two kids.

He stayed in his car, watching. Nobody came or went for a full half hour. It was nothing like the day before.

Brad pulled out the file for his next kill. Kurt hadn't given him much information to go on, but he didn't have to. Not when Brad was usually so good at finding out what he needed to. The car wash made him feel like an amateur. But none of his typical methods yielded anything when it came to this business. Whoever was behind the Slippery Fish was just as careful as BlueBlade.

He made a few notes in the file — he needed to strike fast on this one. And stay off the radar. Someone was going after him when he went out to kill his hits.

And he didn't know if it was someone from his ring or this other one.

Chapter Twenty

BRAD STROLLED through the door with a wide smile. He couldn't wait to tell Hadley the great news about her test results.

Inside was quiet. The salon was empty, which meant the workers were probably at lunch. From the looks of things, they'd finished installing the sinks and painting. There wasn't much left to do.

He couldn't wait for them to be done and leave, taking all the noise with them. Though it was hard to complain with Kurt paying for everything, and considering how fast the crew had pounded through the job. It was unlike anything he'd ever seen.

Brad checked the kitchen, not finding his daughter or mom. They were in the living room, glued to the TV.

"What's going on?"

Hadley turned to him, her face void of color. "The police are pulling something from the harbor."

Brad tried to keep dismay off his face, for Hadley's sake. He'd done everything right with Nate's corpse, so this had to be something else. No point in freaking her out, even for a few minutes. Especially while his mother was in the room.

"A sunken boat from the last storm?" Brad tried to recall if one had gone down recently. Every year, a few reckless people tried their luck, only to discover how unforgiving the waters were.

"Nobody knows." She chewed on a fingernail. "Look."

He sat between them and watched the breaking news. Sure enough, it was as Hadley had said. If the police knew what they were pulling up, they weren't saying. And none of the news cameras showed anything useful. They had angles from the shore, from other boats, and even a helicopter. Yet nobody could see what the authorities were pulling up.

Hadley turned to him. "You don't think they're pulling up ... you know?"

"Not a chance."

"How can you be so sure?"

"Because I am. This is probably just a boat that went down."

"But lots of boats go down, and nobody ever pulls them out." She shivered and wrapped a blanket around herself.

"They do when there's something valuable on it."

"Then why don't they just say that?"

Brad sighed. "It's all about views. That's how they get paid. And a lot more people will tune in if they think it could be a local missing kid."

Hadley frowned.

He turned to his mom. "I got your medications. Do you need any of them now? The pharmacist said you need to take one at lunch."

"I'll have a look. Thanks for picking them up. I know how busy you are."

"Not too busy for you." He pulled out the pill bottles until he found the one to be taken at lunch and showed her.

"Oh, yes. This is a new one. I'd better hurry."

"Do you need any help, Mom?"

She shook her head as she stood. "You've done enough, sweetheart. I can handle my meds."

"Let me at least take them to the table for you."

"You act like I'm a helpless old woman." But she gave him a smile of appreciation.

Once he'd double-checked the medicine against what he found online, he let her take it.

When he returned to the living room, Hadley was curled up in a tight ball, shaking.

He put his arm around her. "I'm telling you, nobody's going to find him."

"How can you be so sure?"

"Because I've done this countless times."

"Something could go wrong. A fish could've bitten off one of his fingers and then someone fishing found it. That would have fingerprints and DNA. Maybe even evidence of me. I can't remember if I—"

"Relax. This has nothing to do with him."

"There's no way to know that! What if someone was scuba diving and they found him?"

Brad drew a deep breath. "It's too far down for a scuba diver, and it's wrapped in too much plastic to be found by a fish. I even poured on a powder that will help it dissolve quicker."

"Not over a weekend."

He shook his head. "No, but I'm telling you, this has nothing to do with him."

Hadley kept shivering.

Brad turned back to the screen, wishing they would just

announce what the police were pulling up. Whatever it was, it wasn't Nate. If it was, then he was the queen of England.

Some reporter was spouting off theories with the police boat in the background. Brad turned it off as soon as she mentioned Nate.

"Hey!" Hadley glared at him.

"Watching this isn't doing you any good. You're supposed to be catching up on schoolwork."

"But they could pull him up any moment!"

"I have some good news."

She blinked a few times. "You do?"

"Yes." He pulled out the paper with her test results and handed it to her.

Hadley looked at the front and back, then held it upside down and sideways. "I don't get it."

"You're clear. You didn't get anything from Nate's blood."

She stared at him for a few moments. "I didn't?"

"Nope. Looks like his reputation was solid." He embraced her. She felt like a rag doll.

"I'm really fine? I'm not going to pass anything onto the baby?"

"You're all good." He leaned back and smiled.

She sighed in relief. "But can they be sure? Did they test for everything? What if some stuff doesn't show until later?"

"They said something about coming back later for another one down the line. Your doctor will give you the details. But take this good news. You deserve it."

"Okay." She sniffled. "Will you put the news back on? I need to know what they find."

He hesitated. "Under two conditions."

"What?"

"First, I want you to promise me you'll stop worrying. Stress will only make you feel worse. Can you do that?"

She frowned.

"I need to hear you agree."

"Fine. What else?"

"Work on your homework while you watch. You're always saying how good you are at multi-tasking. If you can do that, I'll turn it back on."

"Okay." Hadley got up. "I'll get it."

"Thank you."

He turned it back on. The police were still working and the reporters were still making wild guesses.

Brad tried to tell where they were pulling things up, but it was impossible to know if it was the same area where he and Faye had dumped the body. It all looked the same. Lots of water with mountains in the background. It was the harbor. Could be anywhere, really. Without getting on the police boat and checking the coordinates, he wouldn't know.

Hadley returned with her school bag. "Did they say anything new?"

"Still just guessing."

"They haven't pulled anything up?" She plopped on the couch.

"These things take time, especially if it's a big boat."

"So, if it's small like a body, it would be quick?"

"Not necessarily. They might try to be careful, so as not to disturb evidence."

Her shoulders slumped.

Brad regretted saying that. "But probably not this much time. Let me know when they pull up the boat. I'll try to get some work done before the crew comes back."

"Okay."

"I'll be in my office."

"If I hear anything, I'll text you."

"Get your homework done."

"I *know*."

He patted her shoulder before going to the kitchen to check on his mom.

She was busy warming something on the stove.

"Need any help?"

"Just reheating the leftover chili." She smiled at him.

He hated seeing her with the cast, boot, bruises, and stitches. Sometimes he didn't think about it, and other times it hit him how close he'd come to losing her. "Want me to finish that while you rest?"

"No. I need to stretch my legs every so often. Did you know there's a disease that kills people because they sit too much? Crazy the way things change. Back in my day, that was unheard of, because we didn't have five TVs and all those personal devices."

Brad nodded. "True. Well, if you decide you do want my help, just text me. I'll just be doing work."

"I appreciate it. Don't worry about me." She turned back to the stove.

How could he not worry? But she was capable of warming up leftovers, so he trudged upstairs, exhaustion slamming him.

Once in his office, he turned on the news just loud enough to be background noise while he looked into his newest target. Before getting down to business, he did a little digging about the Slippery Fish, but same as before, found nothing.

They really knew how to hide. Not that he was surprised, especially considering how long they'd been in business. BlueBlade's strategy was to have a completely normal online presence, but the car wash was so old, they probably did everything old-school.

He glanced at the TV — some dog food commercial — and got to looking into his target. He was nearly as hard to find information on. Not impossible, but after nearly an hour, Brad had barely found anything. This particular guy could end up being a full-time gig until he got the job done.

If only he knew who had been coming after him. It was easier to blame it on the other assassin ring, but with both Wes and Rose involved in framing him, he couldn't afford to make assumptions. It could be someone from BlueBlade, considering Ralf had refused to tell him how the two were connected.

It might be time to check the dark web. He preferred to do what he could by digging deep into the regular internet, but times like this called for more.

He checked the news again. Whatever the police were drudging up, they were taking their sweet time. Not that he was worried. Even if they were bringing up a body, it couldn't belong to Nate.

He stood and stretched, looked outside.

A streak of blue hair caught his attention. Couldn't that woman leave well enough alone? What was she doing, anyway? Just walking alone along the sidewalk across from the Morris house?

The social worker turned around and walked the same path.

Nothing suspicious there.

She went to the end of the sidewalk before turning around again. Subtlety was clearly not her forte.

Brad had half a mind to go out there and demand answers. But he really needed to find what he could about his target. If he couldn't get anything off the dark web, then he would have to turn to old-fashioned detective work and follow the man. That would require time he didn't have — especially if he didn't want the Bergmanns knowing what he was up to. If they thought he was messing around or focused on his family, all the better.

It would be next to impossible to stalk his target while balancing his job at the knife shop. At least without his bosses clueing in to what he was doing.

No, he had no time to deal with Jacinta Parks. The social worker would have to wait. She had nothing on Hadley — or Brad and Faye for their part in covering up the crime. Otherwise she would have done more than just question them and spend most of her time waltzing around the neighborhood. She was following a hunch. Without proof, she was powerless.

Exactly as he needed her to be.

Brad got onto the dark web and got to work, checking the news and his phone every so often. Hadley and his mom were probably fine downstairs.

It seemed odd that the construction crew hadn't started making their usual noise. They were bound to be back soon enough, and he needed to focus while he could.

His eyelids grew heavy as he clicked around. This was his most challenging case. Almost made him think he'd been given the file of a man who didn't exist.

He sat up straight, his sleepiness gone.

Had he been given a goose chase?

Chapter Twenty-One

ZEKE SLAMMED his notebook shut when the bell finally rang. His classes felt twice as long as normal — and they always dragged.

Wynn grabbed him as he stepped into the hallway. "Did you hear?"

"The school dance was canceled until someone comes forward about the graffiti?"

"No, not that. Who cares about the stupid dance?"

Zeke shrugged. "Not me. I just want to get through my last class."

"Right?" Wynn's eyes lit up. "I can't wait to find out who won the HardCorps event."

"Yeah. That's what I meant."

Wynn shook Zeke's shoulders. "What's with you? *You've* been acting like a zombie all day."

"Shut up." Zeke pulled away. "I need to get to class. Can't be late again, or I get detention. We'll talk later."

"Something's up with you. You can't hide it from me forever."

"I'm not trying to hide anything." Guilt stung. He

never kept anything from Wynn, but what else was he supposed to do? He couldn't tell him top secret information about his dad's job.

"Liar." Wynn stormed off.

Zeke started to call after him, but the warning bell sounded. He would barely have enough time to run to his class if he didn't want to be late.

He slid into his seat just as the bell rang.

What was he supposed to tell Wynn? Everything Dad had said the other night felt like a distant memory. And he didn't want to lie. They'd been best friends forever. Wynn could keep a secret, but this one wasn't Zeke's to tell.

Laughter sounded around him.

He looked up, and the other kids were all looking at him.

"What?"

The teacher tapped his foot. "Didn't hear my question?"

"Guess not."

He marked something in the grade book and turned to a girl in the front row who never answered anything wrong.

A balled-up paper hit the back of his head, followed by snickering.

He stared straight ahead, not wanting to give anyone the satisfaction of seeing him upset.

The next ten minutes went without incident. He even took detailed notes.

Just as they were all turning to page ninety-three in the textbook, the classroom door opened.

A woman he recognized as working in the office stepped in. She looked around. "I need Zeke Morris."

More laughter. Something else struck the back of his head. Felt like an eraser.

The teacher nodded to him and continued the lesson.

Zeke groaned and gathered his things. School was almost over. He wouldn't have to return to class and he'd get the rest of the day off, if he was lucky.

He followed the lady to the office. "Am I in trouble?"

"I don't think so."

"You don't *think*?"

"A social worker has questions for you. That's all I know, dear."

His stomach flip-flopped. Was it the same lady from before? It was like she was stalking them. Showing up at school and their house. Just looking for a reason to pull them in. To get one of them to say they knew where Nate went. Like any of them would know.

"In that room." She pointed to a cracked open door. "She's waiting for you."

Zeke squeezed the strap of his backpack until his fingers hurt. He plodded in, his mouth growing drier by the moment.

The woman with the blue streak in her hair looked up from a table with eight chairs. "I'm Ms. Parks."

"I know."

"Sit, Zeke. We need to talk."

For a moment, Zeke couldn't help wondering if she knew about his dad's secret job, and he was terrified that he wouldn't be able to hide that he knew. That he would forget everything Dad had told him to say.

But how would a social worker know anything about assassination?

He sat as far from her as possible and hoped the rest of the seats wouldn't be filled with people wanting to question him. No way he could take the pressure.

"Do you know why I called you in here?"

Zeke crossed his arms. "To ask me about Nate."

She nodded. "It'll go a lot better for everyone in your family if you would just cooperate."

"We don't know where he is."

"Your sister was the last person to see him."

"No, she wasn't."

Ms. Parks lifted a brow. "No?"

"Kids saw her talking to him after school because they were arguing. But if he was just talking to someone else, nobody probably noticed. And besides, he could've spoken with who knows how many people after he left school. I'm sure if Hadley knew he was going to go missing, she wouldn't have argued with him. You know? It was just bad luck."

"What were they disagreeing about?"

"How would I know?"

"You didn't ask?"

"No." Zeke stared her down.

"Yet you're defending her."

"She's my *sister*."

"Would you protect her if she committed murder?"

"Murder?" His mouth fell open. "Have you met her? She may be perfect and annoying, but she isn't capable of killing anyone. That's crazy."

Ms. Parks made a note on a pad of paper. "I didn't say she did, did I? What I asked was if you'd protect her if she did."

Zeke clenched his fists. "Look. None of us know anything about where Nate went. If you actually want to find him, maybe you should try talking to his real friends. Hadley and I hardly know the guy."

She put her paper down and pressed her hands over it so Zeke couldn't see what she'd written. "Are you aware the police are in the process of pulling something up out of the harbor right now?"

"So?"

"There's speculation that it could be a body."

The walls seemed to close in. "Are you saying it could be Nate?"

She paused a beat before responding. "Could it be?"

"How would I know?"

"*Do* you know?"

"No! Why would I?"

"That's what I'm trying to find out."

"I didn't do anything. Neither did Hadley. She hasn't been feeling good since long before Nate disappeared. Did you know her boyfriend died not long ago?"

"Did she kill him, too?"

Zeke stared at her in disbelief. "Are you serious?"

"People seem to die around your family. Duke, Allison. Maybe Nate."

He wiped his sweaty palms on his jeans. "I'm done talking to you. Don't call me to the office again. Don't come up to me on the street. You're going to have to go through my dad's attorney if you want to talk again."

"You don't need to get upset, Zeke." She gave him a reassuring smile.

He wanted to punch out her perfect teeth.

"I'm completely serious, lady. Don't talk to me again." Zeke grabbed his backpack and raced out of the office.

There was no way he could return to class. Not this upset. Kids would be all over him, making fun of him even worse than usual.

He went to the nearest bathroom and locked himself in a stall. His heart was still racing out of control. That woman was crazy. She could get under his skin like nobody else.

Had she been lying about the police pulling a body out of the harbor?

Zeke pulled out his phone and tried to get one of his apps to load. Most of them didn't work inside the building. The school had some kind of signal jammer, but kids could sometimes get around it.

The third app he tried worked. A search engine. He tapped *police searching Pine Harbor*.

Tons of hits. Most were old. He had to scroll down to find three from that day. He clicked the first article, but the video wouldn't load. He settled on reading it.

The police *were* trying to pull something up, but nobody knew what. Speculations ran wild, including everything from sunken treasure to Nate's body. Zeke had to read that part three times.

Could he really be dead? Zeke had really thought he'd run away. Who could blame him after everything he'd been through? Especially with his aunt wanting to move him away before he had the chance to graduate with his class.

But there were other theories. Maybe the police were looking for a boat that went down, or maybe something that fell from a noncommercial plane. It had to be something like that. What would Nate have been doing down at the harbor?

The bell rang, startling him.

School was over for the day. Noise sounded in the hall as excited kids headed for the buses or after-school activities.

Zeke should join them — he needed to catch his bus — but he couldn't get his legs to cooperate. At this rate, he might spend the whole night in this disgusting stall.

People filled the bathroom. Someone shoved another kid against the stall. Two of the football players made snide comments about Zeke and Wynn. Another kid laughed about the 'stupid' HardCorps competition.

Zeke couldn't take another moment. He flung open the door and marched out, his face hot.

Everyone laughed at him, roaring even louder as he made his escape.

He went to his locker and grabbed the books he needed for homework.

"There you are!" Wynn leaned against the lockers next to him. "I've been looking all over."

Zeke shoved his hands in his pockets so his friend wouldn't see them shaking. "I got called into the office during class."

"What'd you do?"

"Nothing. That social worker keeps asking me about Nate."

"The one with the blue hair?"

"Yeah. Why?"

"She's hot."

"Are you crazy?"

"Come on. Let's get to the bus. I want to get home and find out the winners. We had to have made at least the top hundred. Do you think the top fifty?"

"I didn't get the top one hundred." Zeke slammed his locker shut. "I had too much other stuff to do this weekend."

Wynn shook his head as they started walking. "Family doesn't get it at all. Did my dad's girlfriend friend you?"

Zeke didn't answer right away. He couldn't stop thinking about Nate maybe being dead in the harbor. "Yeah, she did."

"That's so embarrassing. You don't have to accept."

"It's fine." Zeke shrugged.

"Did I tell you my dad made me do some challenges with her? This is so annoying. And I thought the girlfriend who pretended I didn't exist was bad. I'd rather have her back."

"Yeah."

"What's with you? Seriously."

"Nothing."

They stepped into line for their bus.

Wynn shook him. "You have to tell me what's bugging you."

Zeke drew in a deep breath. "Major family drama."

"No kidding. Your sister could have her own reality show."

"You don't know the half of it."

People turned to look at them.

Zeke clenched his jaw. "I don't want to talk about this now."

"Okay. Later, then."

"Yeah."

Wynn rattled on about the famous gamer who everyone thought would get the top rank in the HardCorps competition.

Zeke relaxed a little, glad to have the attention off him for the time being.

Once they sat, that ended.

Wynn turned to him. "So, what's the family drama?"

"I can't talk about it."

"For real?"

"Unfortunately."

"I won't tell anyone. You know me."

"Yeah, but I can't tell anyone."

"Come on. It's *me*."

"I know. But this is major stuff."

"You know I'm not going to say anything. When have I ever let you down?"

Zeke's heart sunk. "Never."

"Then why would I do something stupid now?"

"This doesn't have anything to do with you."

"It affects you."

Zeke sighed.

"Come on. You're going to tell me eventually, anyway. May as well do it now and get it over with."

"I can't. My family is going through some seriously crazy stuff right now."

"All the more reason to talk to me."

Zeke looked outside. They were almost to their stop, and Wynn was still pestering him.

Once out in the cold air, Wynn pulled him away from the other kids. "Are you afraid someone else will overhear? Is that it? It's so loud in there, nobody would've—"

"It's not that. I don't want anyone else hearing, but I just can't tell you. Believe me, I would if I could."

"Then tell me!" Wynn dragged him away from their houses and toward the park. "What is it?"

"I'm not speaking without a lawyer!" Zeke blurted out.

Wynn's eyes widened. He tilted his head. Stared at Zeke.

Zeke looked toward his house, tempted to run and lock himself inside.

"That's the stupidest thing I've ever heard you say to me." Wynn erupted with laughter, doubling over and grasping his stomach.

Zeke's face flamed.

"You need a lawyer to talk to *me*? That's crazy!"

"I'm not crazy!"

Wynn leaned against a tree, still laughing. "You're hilarious!"

"No, I'm not." Zeke marched away.

"Hey, stop!" Wynn grabbed his arm. "What has you acting like a spaz?"

"Nothing. I need to get home."

"All your family ever does is get on your case about things. Do I do that?"

"That's not the point."

"What is it, then?"

"I can't tell you."

"We've established that. Yet we both know you're eventually going to tell me. Why wait?"

The houses around them seemed to grow larger and push closer.

"Well?" Wynn stepped closer.

"My dad's an assassin!"

Wynn just stared.

Zeke brought both hands to his mouth.

What have I done?

Chapter Twenty-Two

Knock, knock, knock, knock, knock, knock!

Brad drew a deep breath and looked up from his desk. "What is it?"

"Dad, it's me!" Zeke called from the other side of the door.

"I'm working."

"This is an *emergency*!" He pounded on the door again.

"Stop knocking! I know you're there."

"Let me in. We have to talk. I did something terrible."

Brad's breath hitched. If he had to hide another body for his children, he would lose his mind.

"Dad!"

He counted to ten before flinging open the door. "What did you do?"

Zeke jumped, his face ashen. The way he stood with his arms wrapped around himself, fidgeting and shaking, made him look like a little boy rather than a teenager.

"Tell me." Brad struggled to keep his voice even. He was already dealing with Hadley, freaking out about the nonstop coverage of the police boat in the harbor.

"You're going to be mad at me. Really mad."

"Just tell me what you did. I can't do anything to help you if you don't."

"I told Wynn."

"You told him what?"

"That you're an assassin." Zeke took a few steps back.

It took Brad a moment to process the news. "Why would you do that?"

"I didn't *mean* to!"

"You just accidentally told him that I kill people."

"He kept asking me what was wrong. I told him over and over that I couldn't tell him. That just made him push more."

"We went over this, Zeke!"

"I *know*. And I tried not to tell him. I even told him I couldn't talk without a lawyer. He laughed at me."

"So, you told him top secret information?"

Every time Brad thought things couldn't spiral further, they did. Now that squirrelly kid down the street knew about him being an assassin. "You know what we have to do now, don't you?"

Zeke gulped. "I don't want to kill him!"

"What? No. I'm not killing a kid. We have to talk to him. Bring him here."

"I ... I—"

"Spit it out!"

"He already went home. To his house."

"Then convince him to come here."

"What if he's scared of you?"

"You'll convince him he has no reason to be worried." Zeke frowned.

"You got us into this mess, now you have to get us out. Bring Wynn here."

"What will I tell him?"

"I'm sure you'll think of something. Make it snappy. Go!"

Zeke's face paled even more, but he headed for the stairs.

Brad paced the hallway, tugging on his hair. He never should've let Faye convince him to tell Hadley. Or they should've at least locked her door during the big reveal. Then Zeke wouldn't have walked in at the exact moment he told her.

Too late to worry about any of that now.

He had to figure out how to keep a neighborhood kid quiet. Considering he hadn't been able to do that with his own son, Brad would definitely have to step it up this time.

He couldn't afford any more mistakes.

Nobody else could find out.

Brad went to the stairs and looked outside. Couldn't see either Zeke or Wynn.

If his son couldn't convince his friend to come over, they had a real problem. Brad's mind roared with possibilities. He didn't want to go over to the kid's house, but it might come down to that. They might have to meet somewhere neutral. Now that he knew the secret, he might worry about coming to the house — he might jump to the same conclusion as Zeke.

But Brad would never hurt a kid. Even if he was given an underage target, he would refuse. He'd never been placed in that situation, but he'd heard rumors of agents who had. The teens had supposedly been as dangerous as their older counterparts, but it was just wrong. They still had a chance to turn their lives around.

Brad went downstairs and looked through every window showing the front of the property. Checked on his mom and daughters — all in the living room. Thankfully, the TV had a cartoon playing. But Hadley was glued to her tablet, which was probably streaming the news.

"Any updates?" he asked.

She shook her head.

"Don't forget your homework. You still want to attempt school tomorrow?"

"I know, and yes."

He asked his mom if she needed anything before returning to the front to look out the window. The doorknob was jiggling like someone was trying to enter after the locks had been changed.

Brad peeked through the window. Zeke and Wynn were on the porch.

Finally.

He opened the door.

Both kids looked like they'd just seen a ghost.

Wynn leaned against the house. "I won't tell anyone, Mr. Morris. You have my word."

"Come inside."

It was hard to say which one was more reluctant to enter.

"What are you going to do, Dad?"

Brad closed and locked the door. "I just want to talk to you kids. Upstairs."

They both trudged up.

Countless thoughts swirled in his head. There wasn't time to say everything he needed to. In order to be effective, he needed to say a few powerful things. Something that would stick, that would keep them both silent.

The boys stopped in front of Zeke's room.

Brad motioned for them to step inside.

"Have a seat."

Both plopped on the bed.

He closed the door and pushed a shelf in front of it.

"Are you going to kill us?" Wynn squeaked.

"Don't be ridiculous."

"But you—"

"I never hurt kids. Ever."

Wynn's arms went visibly limp. "Really?"

"Yes."

Zeke tugged on his hair. "What *are* you going to do?"

Brad paced for a moment, considering his wording. There were so many things he wanted to say, most of which would be too strong for the boys. He wasn't interrogating them for crimes against humanity.

"Dad?"

He spun around and made eye contact with each boy, stopping at Wynn. "Tell me everything you know."

"A-about what you do?"

"Yes."

The boy licked his lips. "I, uh, just what Zeke said."

"Which was what?"

"That you're … you're … you're—"

"Just say it."

"An assassin."

Brad drew a deep breath. Any hopes that the kid had misheard Zeke were out the window. "And you believed him?"

"Not at first." He played with the zipper on his coat. "I laughed at him, thinking he was playing with me. But then I saw the look on his face and knew it was the truth."

"He wasn't supposed to tell you."

"I know. He only did because I wouldn't drop it."

Brad turned to his son. "You aren't going to crumble every time someone asks you about it, are you?"

He shook his head vehemently. "No. I swear. But between the social worker and Wynn—"

"Social worker? You talked to her?"

"She called me out of class."

"Did you refuse to say anything without an attorney?"

"Yes. She kept asking me questions, though. I finally just left."

"Good. Next time, walk away the second you see her. I need to find out who her superior is. But right now, you two are my priority."

"Your secret is safe with me." Wynn pretended to zip his lips. "I've never spilled any of Zeke's secrets. This one won't go anywhere. Telling me something is like telling a brick wall."

Brad studied him for signs of deception.

The kid just appeared nervous.

Not that he could blame him. Brad stepped closer. "You do realize the consequences of saying something, don't you?"

Wynn nodded.

"This is classified information. Not even the police know what I do."

"Did you really kill Duke and Allison?"

"No. Along with kids, I also don't kill people I know. In fact, I refuse to work within the city limits."

"Who *do* you kill?" Wynn leaned forward.

"The worst of the worst. Hardened criminals who have managed to escape the justice system."

"How do they do that?"

"It depends. A lawyer gets them off or they pay their — that doesn't matter. All we need to deal with right now is how to make sure you don't tell anyone."

"I won't. All secrets are safe with me. Just ask Zeke."

Zeke nodded. "It's true."

Brad turned back to Wynn. "What if a police officer demands to know about my job?"

"I won't breathe a word. Zeke's family is my family. I don't spill things, unlike him."

Zeke shoved him.

Brad nodded and stepped closer. "I'm glad to hear that. I need you to understand that your life could be at risk if you do."

"I do."

"The thing is — while *I* won't ever hurt a kid, the same can't be said for the people I work for."

Wynn's mouth gaped.

"While you may know about me, you'll never know who gives me orders. And you don't want to. The moment you meet them, it's over."

"L-lights out?"

Brad nodded slowly. "I know people who have killed kids younger than you two."

Zeke gasped. "For real?"

"Yes. They're also not above killing people's loved ones to get what they want. They might go after you, or they might go after your mom or sister."

Wynn didn't blink.

"I don't want to see that happen. And I know you don't. I'm in this business to keep society safe, but there are many in it for the love of revenge. They have a thirst for blood. Those guys look for reasons to take a life. Even innocent women and children. Maybe even especially them."

Zeke and Wynn exchanged worried looks.

Wynn turned to Brad. "I'll never breathe a word of this to anyone. Ever. I promise."

"I'm glad to hear that. Like I said, killing innocent people isn't something I ever approve of. For me, it's about keeping this world safe. And it is a much better place because of the people I've ... taken care of. Now you have a huge responsibility on your shoulders. It was never my intention for either of you to find out about this. Any questions before you go home?"

He squirmed. "So, basically, if I stay quiet, then my family stays safe?"

"Precisely. You and your family."

Wynn swallowed. "Understood."

Brad pulled a business card from his pocket. "If you have any questions, call me. I don't care what time it is."

Wynn took the card and put it in his jacket.

"Go home and spend some time with your family. Say nothing."

"Th-thanks."

He patted Wynn's shoulder and smiled at Zeke.

With any luck, this was a crisis averted. But Brad wasn't a fool. He'd have to keep a close eye on both of the boys now.

Chapter Twenty-Three

Zeke pulled his jacket tighter and shivered. "Sure you don't want to go inside?"

Wynn shook his head. "No. This is our only chance to talk without anyone around."

"We don't have to go to the cafeteria." Zeke looked inside at all the kids in the warm building eating their lunches.

"Someone could overhear us." Wynn looked around for the five-hundredth time. "We can talk freely here."

"Or we could go to my house after school."

"I couldn't sleep all night and I still can't eat. I'm not risking anyone overhearing us. Someone could be after my family! Or me."

"I know."

"Why did you have to tell me about your dad's job?"

Zeke looked at him like he was crazy. "Seriously?"

"Yeah. You should've told me to shove it."

"What about you telling me that I could trust you? That there were no secrets between us. I kept telling you no."

"You should've stuck to your guns. Now my life is in danger."

"Maybe learn to trust people when they say no."

Wynn narrowed his eyes. "And maybe you should learn to keep a secret."

"You're impossible."

"And you're dangerous! I never thought you'd do this to me. If you'd have told me it was life and death, I'd have listened."

"Would you?"

"Yes!"

Zeke grabbed his backpack and flung over his shoulder. "That's it. I'm going inside."

"Wait."

He didn't stop.

Wynn caught up with him. "Okay, okay. This isn't your fault. I wasn't going to give up until you told me. Even if you'd have said it was a matter of national security, I'd have pushed until you broke."

"Then stop blaming me." Zeke picked up his speed, eager to get out of the cold rain.

"I can't help being freaked out. This is insane! Your dad kills people for a living."

"You think I don't know that? I'm still trying to wrap my head around it myself." He flung open the door and took in the warmth. "We're done talking about this until later. You can come to my house after school if you want."

"I will."

Zeke's stomach rumbled, but there wasn't enough time to get in line and sit down to eat. He'd just have to wait until later.

"Uh-oh. Here comes trouble."

"Who?" Zeke looked around.

"Elena at two o'clock."

He glanced over to see Nate's sister heading their way. "What does she want?"

"Probably to ask you more questions about her brother. You didn't kill him, did you?"

Zeke shoved Wynn into a locker. "Don't even joke about that."

"Overreact much?"

"Am I interrupting anything?" Elena's eyes were full of judgment.

"What do you want?" Zeke grumbled.

"I want to find out where my brother is."

"And you think we know?"

She narrowed her eyes. "You and your sister are his friends."

"You keep using that word. I do not think it means what you think it means."

"The two of you hung out with him!"

"Like one time. Because we happened to run into him. If that's what you call friendship, you live a sad life."

Elena glared at him. "Hadley was arguing with him before he disappeared."

"Your point?"

"She should've been nicer to him. Our mom died and our dad is in jail. Now our aunt is moving us away from all of our friends. The last thing he needed was one of his friends treating him like that."

"Stop using that word." Zeke glowered at her. "If you want to talk to Hadley, talk to *her*. I don't know anything about Nate."

"Your sister keeps missing school. Coincidence?"

"Yes! She hasn't been feeling good. But she's there today."

Elena squared her shoulders. "Fine. I'll talk to her myself."

"What's up with the social worker?"

"She's trying to find Nate. What's wrong with that?"

"Tell her to leave me alone. I don't know anything."

"Whatever."

Zeke stormed away. Between the social worker and Elena, he couldn't take any more. It was all too much. It might not be so bad if he wasn't dealing with the new knowledge of his dad's real career.

Wynn caught up with him. "She's really focused on your family."

"We're easy targets. Her dad drilled it into their heads that my dad killed their mom — when *he* was the murderer."

"Do you think he did it?"

"No. Wes is in jail."

"I mean Nate."

"He just ran away."

"But what if he didn't?" Wynn tilted his head.

"Not you, too." Zeke headed for his locker.

"Think about it."

"We've already been over this. He doesn't want to move away his senior year. Who would?"

"But what if your dad *did* do it?"

Zeke glowered at his friend. "We shouldn't talk about this here at school."

"So, you want to wait until we get home. Your place or mine?"

"I've already got that social worker and Elena on my case about this. I don't need you, too. If you think he did it, then call him. You've got the card."

"Okay, okay." Wynn held up his hands. "Understood."

"Thank you."

The warning bell sounded, and they parted ways.

Zeke checked his bag to see if he needed to stop by his

locker for anything. He didn't have the textbook for his next class, so he hurried to get it.

Just before slamming the locker shut, a conversation on the other side caught his attention.

"—body in the harbor."

Zeke's heart skipped a beat. Did the police actually find a body? Was that what they'd been searching for? Or were the kids just speculating?

"It's on this blog," said a girl.

"That site is all gossip."

"Not always."

"Yeah, always."

Zeke checked the time — he'd have to run if he wanted to make it on time. He slammed the locker shut and bolted, making it to his seat just as the final bell rang.

The teacher gave him a warning look before telling everyone what page to open to.

Zeke followed instructions, paying closer attention to the whispers around him. Some gossip about a cheerleader kissing someone from chess club. A couple of kids busted for smoking. Nothing about the police in the harbor.

He forced his attention back to the teacher and the lesson. It was hard to focus. Nearly impossible.

What if the police *had* found a body? And what if his dad *did* have something to do with it? He'd been lying all these years about being an assassin, what would keep him from lying about this, too?

He would have to ask him straight out. See how he responded to the question.

But what if he admitted to it? Said that it was payback for everything Wes had done to him? Then what?

Zeke shuddered at the thought. Maybe not knowing was better. Just believing that Dad was telling the truth about not going near anyone local.

Zeke hurried out when the period finally ended, eager to be done with the day. But he still had another class before he could make his beeline for the bus and lose himself in HardCorps.

He skidded to a stop.

The social worker was standing in a corner behind the crowd of kids. Her focus was on Zeke. She didn't even look away when he made eye contact.

She wanted him to know she was watching.

Did she know what the police had found?

Chapter Twenty-Four

BRAD WAVED GOODBYE TO GARY, eager to take in the silence. They were officially done with the work on Faye's salon. The noise had felt like it lasted decades, but the work got done in record time. If Brad had hired a crew, it would have easily taken three times as long.

It paid to have connections. But now Kurt would expect him back at work, as soon as Faye quit the salon. Brad would refuse to come in a minute sooner, because someone had to stay with his mom.

Unless Kurt got so desperate for Brad to return that he hired a day nurse for his mom. But why would he want Brad back so badly? Wasn't his next target the most important thing? He could better prepare for the hit at home.

He checked on his mom, who was out in the backyard with Bingo. Then he looked at his phone. No messages or calls from Hadley. She must be doing well at school. At least that was what he was going with — no news was good news.

Now he could get back to work. He'd made great progress on his target, finding everything he needed on the dark web. Best of all, Brad hadn't needed to question Kurt about any of it. The more he kept his boss out of things, the better.

For his previous hits, Kurt knew everything, and Brad had himself been targeted.

Not this time.

He would go after his man on his own.

If someone went after him, then he would have reason to worry. That would mean someone was watching him closely — and somehow, he'd failed to notice.

This was his only way of figuring out for sure if someone in his company was consigning the hits on him. Twice in a row was too much to be coincidence.

Once his mom and Bingo came in, he helped settle her on the couch with a movie. That would give him two hours of uninterrupted work.

In silence.

He couldn't help smiling at that thought.

Brad marched up the stairs, enjoying the sounds of his footsteps. He glanced through the window into the now-ready salon. Faye would be thrilled when she got home. He nearly texted her the good news, but wanted to see her expression.

Besides, he had two hours to himself.

He settled into his desk chair and flipped through his notes. Part of his preparation, once he'd gathered all the info, was to look for what he might have missed and what assumptions he could have possibly made.

He needed to kill this guy before Kurt started asking questions.

Brad picked up a box of things from his father's office he'd been meaning to go through. The first thing he pulled out was a ledger book. It appeared to record the items his dad had purchased for his assassinations and trainings. Everything in it aligned with Brad's own experience.

He checked for any discrepancies — anything that would have been a hidden code — but saw nothing out of place. It really did seem to be an account of business purchases.

Brad set that aside and grabbed another book. Cryptic notes on targets. Decoding Dad's abbreviations got easier after he figured out the first few. He skimmed, looking for anything that might point to the lead-up to his dad's murder. Clues his dad had picked up on, or even missed but noted by accident.

Hopefully, the answer was in one of the books now in Brad's office.

Going through the rest of the box yielded nothing beyond the usual admin stuff, except that instead of Blue-Blade, Slippery Fish was the company mentioned.

Brad hoped that his loved ones wouldn't be going through his notes looking for clues to his death one day. He shoved that thought aside, replaced the books, and grabbed another box he'd not yet had time to go through.

Before pulling out the first book — another accounts ledger — he crept downstairs to check on his mom. She was too enthralled in her movie to notice him.

Back in his office, he kept the door wide open and flipped through a few more books. Again, more of the same. Nothing suspicious. No clues pointing to Dad's murderer.

Time ticked by as he went through each of the ledgers. He went downstairs and helped his mom find another movie. But the quiet house would only last so long. The kids would be home from school soon.

He checked the time. Seemed like Hadley should've been back by now. Maybe she was busy catching up with her friends, or perhaps she still had her part in the school play and was at rehearsal.

Zeke was definitely due soon. At least he would want to hole himself up in his room to play his game.

Brad had never appreciated a video game more than at that moment.

He left his door cracked open and dug back into his search, still finding nothing of interest.

But then his breath hitched as his hands fell on a different sort of book, what looked like some sort of journal. Was it an actual diary, or simply filled with more numbers and facts, much of it in code? If Brad hadn't been in the business himself, he wouldn't have been able to figure out as much as he already had.

The door slammed downstairs.

He nearly dropped the journal, but managed to catch the volume and set it gently on the desk. Then he went to the staircase to see who was home.

Zeke and Wynn kicked off their shoes in the living room, whispering to each other.

So much for his cherished silence.

"Everything okay?" Brad asked.

Zeke looked up. "Yeah. We're just gonna get a snack and play HardCorps."

"Hey, Mr. Morris, did you hear anything about what the police are looking for in the harbor?" Wynn asked.

"No. Have you?"

"Kids are whispering about a body."

"I wouldn't know anything about that." He went down a few steps. "Zeke, offer your grandma a snack, would you?"

"Sure."

Brad went back to his office and listened to the police scanner. Nothing about the harbor. Checked the news sites and didn't see anything new. Not that it mattered. Nobody would find Nate's body.

He returned to his father's journal, his hands shaking as he turned to the first page.

It was crazy to think that he might find the answers here, but he couldn't shake the hope. Somebody knew something, and one of the entries in this book might provide a clue to that person's identity.

The murderer had been walking around free for three decades. He or she had to believe that they'd never be caught.

Brad wanted to be there when the killer discovered it was time to pay.

He reined in his thoughts. No point in daydreaming about retribution when he didn't know what secrets this journal held. It could be artwork for all he knew.

The first page had his dad's name and a date. Brad did the mental math — just under four months ahead of his death.

He flipped to the next page. A journal entry.

His dad wrote about one of the other assassins turning against him out of jealousy, apparently resenting that he'd moved up so quickly in the company. The other guy, unnamed, was a young man, barely twenty. Same reason that Rose had given, and it felt weak here too.

Brad skimmed through the entries. The further along he read, the more convinced his dad had become that the young guy was a threat — not only to his career, but to his life.

He knew the murder was coming. Or at the very least, he saw it as a very real possibility.

Why hadn't he identified his rival?

Brad's pulse quickened. Could it be someone he'd seen at the car wash? Brad was sixteen at the time of the murder. That would put the killer at about four to six years older than Brad.

Had someone at the Slippery Fish over the weekend been that age? Someone like that could've easily gotten himself killed. If not during a mission, then something like the Felix incident. So were they even alive?

Brad's revenge might very well be out of reach.

He strained to remember everyone he'd seen the other day. It certainly hadn't been the pair of kids he'd spoken with. Neither of them would've been alive. Ralf was too old, plus he didn't work at the wash.

Brad would have to spend more time staking out the Slippery Fish. Keep going through his father's old things in search of names. The problem was how well Dad had coded everything. How was he going to figure out the real names of the people who'd worked there thirty years earlier?

Laughter came from down the hall, pulling Brad from his thoughts. He got up to close his door.

The journal pages flipped to the middle of the book.

A name caught his attention, as if it were blinking in neon.

Brad read and re-read the paragraph.

His dad had been sure that person was out to get him, to take him down.

He described him as a young man rising in the ranks whose sister had been murdered.

Kurt Bergmann was his enemy.

There were no more entries after this one on the day of his death.

Chapter Twenty-Five

Brad stepped inside, tossing the empty beer bottle into the patio bin. His mind was still spinning, but at least he'd made it past the initial shock. He'd re-read Dad's last journal entry at least a dozen times, making sure he'd read it right. Snapped pictures on his phone and made paper copies.

No way would he risk something like that going missing.

"You okay?" Faye looked at him with concern from the kitchen stove.

"Yeah."

"What were you doing outside? You're soaked."

Brad looked at his flannel. It was dripping onto the floor. "I'll clean that up."

"I'm more concerned about you."

He wanted to tell her, but what if Kurt stopped by the house to see how the salon turned out? He doubted Faye would be able to hide her feelings if she knew the truth — then Kurt would know that Brad was onto him.

He might never get the chance to avenge his father.

"It's some work stuff. I just need to get through it."

She lifted a brow. "You sure that's all it is?"

"Yes. Something to do with Kurt. You don't need to worry about it."

Her eyes brightened. "Speaking of him, give him a hearty thanks for me. I couldn't be more thrilled about how the home salon turned out. It's gorgeous!"

Right. He'd wanted to see her expression when she got her first glimpse. Too late now.

Maybe it was better that way. It was hard enough hearing her gratitude for his father's killer. "I'll be sure to tell him you like it."

She stepped away from the stove and studied him. "Something's wrong. What is it?"

"Just work stuff," he repeated. "Nothing for you to worry about."

Faye frowned.

Brad gave her a kiss. "It's fine, really. Thanks for making dinner. I'll be down to help with the dishes in—"

"Don't worry about it. It's Zeke's turn today."

"I'll let him know." Brad hurried upstairs and told Zeke to help his mom in the kitchen.

Noise sounded from his office, and the door was cracked open.

Brad's heart plummeted.

Had Kurt found out about the journal and broken in?

No. That was crazy.

He burst inside, flinging the door against the wall.

Hadley looked up from his desk, her eyes wide and mouth gaping.

"What are you doing in here?" Brad demanded.

"The door was open, so I came in to listen to the scanner. I won't do it again." She jumped up and headed for the door.

He stopped her gently. "You're fine. I didn't realize I left it unlocked. I should be more careful. Did you hear anything?"

She shook her head, tears shining in her eyes. "I can't stop thinking about it."

"I know you're worried, but I'm telling you the cops aren't going to find anything."

"It isn't just that."

"What, then?"

Hadley blinked the tears onto her face. "I *killed* him."

Right. Of course she'd be upset about that. It was her first — and hopefully only — one. She'd had no training, nothing preparing her for the train wreck of emotions.

He held her close. "Do you want to talk about it?"

"How's that going to help?"

"The same way counseling does. Only this is free."

She frowned.

"I've been through this, honey. Let me help."

"You can't help. Nothing will bring him back. If they do find him, then I deserve to go to jail. Especially for hiding it. I should've called the police when it happened."

Brad motioned for her to sit back down in his chair, then pulled up another one for himself. "You did the right thing by coming to us. It was a mistake, and he was threatening you. There's no reason your life should be ruined because of one moment where you were scared for your life."

How many times would he have to say it before she believed him?

She wiped her eyes. "He wasn't threatening my *life*."

"No, but your reputation. Also, you wouldn't have had the knife on you in the first place if you hadn't been concerned for your safety."

"That was because of his dad."

"And the apple doesn't fall far from the tree. You did what you needed to do."

"You're a terrible counselor."

"Why?"

"Because you don't ask any questions. All you're trying to do is fix things. Fix me."

He sighed. "I can't stay neutral. You're my daughter."

"How am I supposed to live like this? Will the guilt ever go away?"

"Yes. It'll get better with time. You have the added pressure of worrying about getting caught. But I'm telling you, that isn't going to happen."

"They're searching the harbor!"

"Even if they are looking for him — which nobody can prove, it's all speculation at this point — they won't find him."

Silence rested between them for several long seconds. "What would you tell me if I was someone you were training?"

"That the person you took care of deserved it, and the world is now a better place because of your bravery."

Her mouth wavered and more tears shone in her eyes. "But that isn't true. Not for me."

"Maybe it is. What if Nate would've ended up like his dad in the long run? Then you've saved other women's lives."

Hadley shook her head.

"Don't think so?"

"He wouldn't kill anyone. Unlike me."

"Nate was on the path to becoming like his dad. And who knows how many other women Wes killed besides his wife?"

Her expression tightened. "Wes was involved in Duke's

death. They just didn't pin it on him. Rose took the fall, but I heard them talking."

"That's true."

Hadley held his gaze. "Was he an assassin, too? Or did Rose just pull him in to help her with Duke?"

Brad hesitated. Admitting that Wes was also an assassin could lead Hadley to thinking she would eventually become a killer, too.

Ding-dong!

He leaped up and looked out the window. No car in sight, but their visitor might have parked on the other side where he couldn't see. He turned back around.

"Who is it?" Hadley wiped her eyes.

"I'm not sure."

"Brad!" Faye called from downstairs. "It's the social worker!"

His muscles tightened. "Don't answer it."

She appeared in the doorway. "Too late, your mom let her in."

He closed his eyes for a moment, trying to recover his strength. "I'll be right down."

Hadley wrapped her arms around herself. "What about me?"

"Stay here and keep listening to the scanner. See if they mention anything about Jacinta Parks. I don't think she's working with them, but I'd like to know if I'm wrong."

"Okay. But who else would she be working for?"

"The family. Maybe Wes is behind this. She's far too pushy, and I don't trust her. The police weren't this bad when looking for Duke or Allison's killers."

Hadley chewed on a fingernail. "But he's a missing kid. Maybe that's more urgent."

"Just listen to the scanner. They'd probably mention

her if she's working with them. The way she's acting, we're all prime suspects."

Faye gave Hadley a kiss, then left the room, taking Brad's hand as they descended the stairs. "You really think she's working apart from the police?"

"I'd bet on it."

Downstairs, the social worker was studying a picture of the family, taken two years earlier.

"Can we help you?" Brad asked.

Jacinta turned to him. "Nate has been missing for nearly a week—"

"It hasn't been that long already, has it?" Brad knew full well it wasn't.

"I said *almost*. We're well past the critical twenty-four-hour mark, and we don't have any other clues."

"And yet you keep wasting time on my family. Why is that?"

"Everything keeps coming back to your household."

"Is it a crime to argue with someone at school?" Brad stepped closer to Jacinta.

"It's suspicious."

"People suspected me in the deaths of Duke Hill and Allison Campbell. But as it turned out — innocent as a dove in both cases."

Jacinta snorted.

"You don't think so?"

"You're no dove."

He furrowed his brows and stepped even closer, leaving barely any space between them. "What are you getting at?"

Jacinta didn't back down. "You know something about Nate."

"Really? What do I know?"

"That's what I'm trying to find out."

"Why is it that *you* are the one investigating this, and not the police? I'd think that if they suspected me or my family, Detective Stewart would be all over this. And yet, I haven't seen her since all of this began."

"I can't speak for the police force."

"That proves my point. You need to leave now."

Her nostrils flared. "It's obvious that Nate met with some trouble. One or both of your kids knows something. They—"

"You have no proof about anything. You need to take *legal* action, and I've already warned you to stay away from my children. Do I need to call my attorney? I have his number right here." Brad reached for his pocket.

"No need for that." Her face went red. "I'll leave, but don't think for a moment that this is over."

Brad opened the door and waited for her to leave. "Buh-bye."

She glared at him before stepping outside.

He slammed the door and locked it behind her. "If she comes by again, call the cops."

Faye nodded.

Hadley appeared at the top of the stairs, her eyes wide.

Brad's stomach sank to the floor. "Did you hear something on the scanner?"

She shook her head. "I got a text from Norah."

"Who?"

"That snob I hit last week in the school bathroom. Her dad's a lawyer, and she's threatening a lawsuit."

"A *lawsuit?*" Brad exclaimed. "For one punch?"

"She had it coming."

"I don't doubt it." He rubbed his temples. "Forward me her number, or her father's, if you have it. I'll put an end to this."

What was one more thing on his plate?

Chapter Twenty-Six

BRAD ENDED the call and drew a deep breath. It was exactly as he'd expected. The brat's father had no idea his daughter was threatening Hadley with a lawsuit. In fact, he hadn't even known about her being punched — that's how "bad" it had been. He was aware of his daughter provoking other kids at school and threatening them with court, but knew nothing of Hadley's instance. He promised to deal with Norah as long as Brad agreed to discuss the seriousness of assault with Hadley.

At least that was one crisis averted. Now there was the matter of making sure Hadley stayed off the radar of everyone who was looking for Nate.

Then he needed to deal with Kurt.

The thought boiled his blood. He'd been working for the man for over a decade, trusted him with his life. And he'd murdered Brad's dad?

Then he'd taken Brad under his wing. Mentored him. Kurt was the reason he had become an assassin.

Was that supposed to be some kind of sick joke?

Or Kurt's last act of revenge against his father?

His stomach lurched, but he managed to keep his dinner down.

It made *everything* look different now. Had Kurt merely been trying to keep Brad close to divert him from finding the truth? Was it all a ruse to cover his own crime?

Or had his dad gotten it all wrong? He hadn't left any more journal entries, so there was no way to know.

Whether his dad was right about Kurt was hard to say, but he'd been right about someone wanting him dead. But why? What had he done? His dad had been a family man, always doing the right thing. Even the assassination business was about making things right.

Why would Kurt want to kill him? Had it been something like Brad's issue with Rose? The young assassin jealous of his mentor? That seemed to be the only thing that made any sense, at least until he knew more.

Before Duke was killed and Brad was implicated in the death, Brad had spoken with Kurt about looking into his dad's murder. Why wouldn't he? He'd had no reason to think his dad had also been in the assassin business. No reason to believe Kurt had ever met his old man, much less taken his life.

That was when everything went south — two men had attacked Brad while he went after his assigned target. But he hadn't anticipated Brad taking his attackers down.

Then Duke had died — the one neighbor everyone knew Brad had an ongoing feud with. Whether Kurt knew about Hadley's relationship with the victim was up for debate, but it made him look all the guiltier.

And when none of those efforts managed to take down Brad, Allison was murdered. Another neighbor who Brad openly didn't like. He was an easy suspect, especially after much of the neighborhood had presumed his involvement in Duke's death.

With Wes working for the Slippery Fish, it made it all the easier for Kurt to make that killing happen. Given the problems he'd been having with Allison, Wes had probably been more than willing.

He just hadn't anticipated getting caught. Now he was in jail and Brad was still a free man.

But how much longer would that last? Would his boss continue pinning murders on him until he was finally arrested?

It wasn't out of the realm of possibility. Brad had to consider that it might not be Kurt. It often helped to look into other cases when researching a current target.

And of course, Ralf had access to everything.

Brad's phone rang, and he jumped.

It was Kurt.

He stared at it for a moment before answering. "Brad here."

"Hey, it's Kurt. Has Faye seen her new salon yet?"

Brad's mind went blank.

He needed to focus. To stay at the top of his game. Not let Kurt figure out that he was onto him.

"Are you still there?" Kurt asked.

"My connection is kind of spotty. The construction crew did a phenomenal job, and so quickly, too."

"Great. That's what I wanted to hear. And how are things going with your hit? You haven't checked in with any details."

"He's a tough man to find anything on. I hate to say it, but I might need some extra time for this one."

"Really? My top guy?" There was a slight hint of sarcasm in his voice, but it was buried underneath the now obviously-artificial friendliness.

"I'm sure things would be different if I wasn't dealing with my mom's life-threatening health issues and all the noise from the construction — not that I'm complaining."

"Plus, your oldest is having some issues."

"Right." Brad gritted his teeth, wanting to ask how much he knew. "There's a lot on my plate."

"Sure you still want to make the hit? I can give it to—"

"I've got it. I'll just need a little extra time. Shouldn't be too much more now that the construction's done. I can focus better."

"What about coming into the shop? When will that happen?"

"I need to find out when Faye can open her salon. She's required to give a certain amount of notice. I forget how much, exactly."

"You don't know?"

Brad forced a laugh. "Do you know all the details of MaryAnne's life?"

"You bet I do."

His skin bristled.

Kurt laughed. "Kidding, of course. I can barely keep up with whether she's getting her nails done or playing tennis at the club. Talk to Faye, and let me know. Just don't take too long. This target has to go down soon. If you can't get to him, I need someone else to do it."

"You can trust that I'm on it."

"Glad to hear. Be in touch by tomorrow morning."

"Will do."

They said goodbye, and Brad squeezed the arms of his chair. At least Kurt hadn't seemed to notice anything off.

But that still didn't give him much time to eliminate his target without alerting Kurt.

If an assassin showed up, then Brad would know Kurt was trying to kill him for looking into his dad's murder.

It was time to finish the job.

Chapter Twenty-Seven

ZEKE PULLED off his headphones and stretched, yawning. It felt later than he was usually allowed to play on a weeknight.

He glanced at the time. Quarter after ten. Strange that Dad hadn't demanded he go to bed yet.

Maybe he was busy with Grandma. Or distracted by Hadley. She might be freaking out about Duke again, or her baby. Could be anything with her.

He headed for the bathroom to brush his teeth, stopping outside Dad's office. It was locked as usual, but the light was off. If he wasn't in there, where was he? The door to his parents' bedroom was also closed and dark.

Instead of brushing his teeth, Zeke headed downstairs. Mom was in her salon, painting something on one of the walls. *Material Girl* sounded from the other side.

Zeke nodded in approval — not that it was his first choice in 80s music — before following TV noise to the living room, where Grandma was watching a black-and-white show.

She turned and smiled at him. "Can I get you a snack, sweetie?"

"No, thanks. Have you seen Dad?"

"He went to work for a few hours. Said not to wait up for him."

"Now?" Zeke double-checked the time.

Ten-twenty.

Grandma nodded and turned back to the screen. "Want to watch this with me? Dick Van Dyke is so funny. You'll really like this show."

"Maybe next time. I have to get to bed for school tomorrow."

He headed back upstairs, and stared at the office door. His pulse quickened as he imagined that his father might be taking a life at this very moment.

How was this his reality now? It had been for years, but now he could never unknow it.

Zeke tiptoed back down the stairs.

Mom was still busy working on her wall.

He didn't want to interrupt her, but he needed to talk to someone.

His gaze landed on Hadley's door.

It was her or nobody. Wynn wasn't allowed calls this late on school nights.

Zeke's stomach knotted even tighter, his hands growing clammy as he knocked on her door.

"Come in," she called.

His moist hand slid off the knob, and he fumbled before finally opening the door.

"Forget how doors work?" Hadley said from behind her laptop.

"Shut up. You earned back your devices."

She made a face at him. "What do you want?"

"Do you know where Dad is?"

She shrugged. "In his office?"

Zeke shook his head, waiting for her to figure it out.

"I'm not playing guessing games. I'm behind on this essay."

His stomach lurched. "He's killing someone."

Hadley's laptop started to fall off her lap. She grabbed it. "What are you talking about?"

"He's *at work*."

She glanced at her screen. "This late?"

"Uh huh."

"Maybe he's doing something else."

"Like what?"

"I don't know. I need to get back to my paper. Talk to you later."

Zeke closed the door behind him and leaned against it. "I'm not going anywhere. Doesn't it freak you out? He could be killing someone right this second."

Her eyes narrowed. "You know, killing isn't as horrible as you're making it out to be."

"Are you crazy?"

"No!" One side of her mouth curved down. "Dad said he only kills bad guys. People who deserve it."

"So? It's still killing. Taking a life." His voice cracked. "And this is *Dad* we're talking about."

"Yeah, and he's making this world a safer place. Getting people like Wes off the streets."

"Wes *is* off the streets."

"Dad isn't a bad guy. He's doing something most people couldn't do, and he can't even tell anyone. He wasn't supposed to tell us."

"But he did tell you."

"And that's why you should learn to knock." Hadley raised her eyebrows.

"This whole thing makes me feel like I'm going to yak."

"That's not my fault."

"I can't believe you don't even care!"

"Of course I do — I don't want you spewing in here. And besides, if you do, I probably will, too. Last thing I need is a matching set of piles to deal with."

Zeke glowered at her. "How can you take this so lightly?"

"I'm not. Vomit's gross."

"Is there something I don't know?"

"Like what?" Hadley asked.

"There has to be a reason Dad told you about his real job. Why?"

"Go away! I need to finish my homework."

Zeke stepped closer to her. "Why did he tell you?"

"I don't know! Leave me alone." Hadley closed her eyes and drew a deep breath. "Would you please just go?"

Zeke waited until she opened her eyes. "I know you're hiding something."

"I'm pregnant with our dead neighbor's child. What else do you think I'm hiding?"

"I don't know, but I'm going to find out."

"Anything to keep your mind off dad's job. Have fun. At least you'll be out of my hair."

"I'm going to be *more* in your hair until I figure out what you're keeping secret." Zeke spun around and stormed across the room. Just as he touched the knob, she spoke.

"You wouldn't."

"I won't give up until I find out — and I will. I promise you that."

Her glare softened to a frown.

She might tell him.

His heart thundered. He almost had her. "Come on, Hadley. I'm your *brother*. We're family. If we can't be here for each other, who can be here for us? Really."

She looked like she was considering it.

"I wouldn't tell anyone. Blood is thicker than water."

Her expression softened even more. "This is as big as Dad's secret. Maybe bigger."

He slowly walked closer. "Bigger?"

Hadley's face was pale. She nodded.

Zeke stumbled the rest of the way over. "For real?"

She grabbed his wrist and squeezed. Hard. "You can't tell *anyone*."

"I won't." He tried to free his hand.

Her grip tightened. "I'm serious. This is even bigger than everything with Duke."

"You already made that clear."

"If you tell anyone I'll kill you."

"Okay." He yanked his arm away. "I won't breathe a word of this. I swear."

She rolled her eyes. "That's reassuring."

"You can trust me. What's your big secret?"

Hadley chewed on her lip and motioned for him to sit. "I'm only going to tell you because I need someone to talk to about this that isn't Mom and Dad, and I can't tell any of my friends."

He plopped down next to her, his heart racing in anticipation of her juicy secret. Too bad he wouldn't be able to tell Wynn. No way would he risk that picture getting out. No matter how many times someone asked.

"What is it?"

Hadley looked back and forth between him and her nails. "Maybe I shouldn't."

"You can't do this to me! Not after all that."

She frowned. "I shouldn't have said anything."

"You *haven't*."

Hadley twisted some hair around her finger, tightly enough to turn the digit white. Tears shone in her eyes as she finally confessed. "I killed Nate."

Time froze.

Zeke stared at his sister in disbelief. "What did you say? Because it sounded like you said you killed Nate."

She blinked, and a tear rolled down her cheek. The color had returned to her skin, and she looked relieved. "It was an accident — I didn't mean to. It just sort of happened."

It felt like he was floating. "You ... you really killed him?"

She nodded.

Nate, his friend, was gone forever. Not just missing, but dead. Killed by his sister.

Tears streamed down her face. "I didn't want to! He wouldn't leave me alone, and he was threatening me."

Heat rose in Zeke's chest, and he clenched his fists. "He was threatening you?"

"Yeah. He wouldn't stop, and I had a knife." She wiped her eyes. "It's all a blur, but then suddenly there was blood all over and he wasn't moving."

"Why are you telling me this?" His stomach lurched and he covered his mouth.

"I hated keeping it in! All these secrets are driving me crazy. I can't tell my friends any of this. I just can't."

"It isn't just you — but Dad? You're both killers."

"Mine was an accident." She stared at him. "I didn't mean to."

Zeke scooted over to lean against the wall, no longer able to support his own weight. "What did you do with the body?"

She looked away.

"What?" he demanded.

"This is the part I shouldn't tell you."

Zeke threw his arms in the air. "I don't think I can deal with any more of your secrets. I wish I'd never insisted you tell me this one." He drew a deep breath. "Don't tell me."

But just as he said that, Hadley spoke. "Mom and Dad took care of it. Dad says nobody will ever find it."

"They know?" he exclaimed, though nothing should shock him by now.

"You won't tell anyone, will you?"

"And have my entire family carted off to prison? No way."

Hadley sighed in relief. "Thank you."

"Mom and Dad know, and they *covered* for you?"

She just nodded.

Unreal. His sister literally got away with murder. Well, an accidental killing. Close enough. And their parents covered it up.

And he got in trouble for spending too much time playing HardCorps.

He turned back to Hadley. "So, what now? Everything goes back to life as normal?"

"I guess. But I can't stop thinking about it. I have nightmares, and I see him when I'm awake, too." Her eyes shone with tears, and her lips quivered. "He was my friend. I never wanted to hurt him. How am I supposed to deal with that?"

Zeke squirmed. He never knew what to do when girls cried. And Hadley wouldn't stop looking at him as if expecting answers. He cleared his throat. "Have you asked Dad? I'm sure he knows more about this than I do."

She leaned against his shoulder. "He's no help. It's just another day at the office for him."

"Literally."

Hadley nodded and sniffled. "I keep waiting for that social worker to figure something out, or for the police to pull Nate from the harbor."

Zeke pushed himself away from the wall. "*That's* why you guys have been freaking out about that? Mom and Dad put him there?"

She wiped her nose. "Yeah, but Dad swears they'll never find him. Says they're looking for something else out there."

He climbed off the bed. "This is too much. I need to go to bed. Maybe when I wake up, all of this will turn out to be a bad dream."

"I wish."

Zeke took unsteady steps back to the door. But halfway there he was struck by a thought. He whipped back around. "What if we have the killer gene in our family? That means I could end up killing someone, too!"

"There's no such thing as a killer gene."

"Yes, there is! Don't you watch TV?"

"It's called *fiction*. It's fake. Go to bed."

Like she knew what she was talking about.

He would never get any sleep that night. Not knowing that his friend was dead and two members of his family were killers — and apparently cool with that.

What if it was only a matter of time before Zeke took someone's life, too?

Chapter Twenty-Eight

BRAD SET down his dad's journal and smiled, thinking about how well the previous night's killing had gone. He'd taken out his target without any interruptions. It had almost been too easy.

Funny how when he kept Kurt out of the loop, things worked out so differently.

His phone rang.

He jumped, he'd been so lost in his thoughts.

It was Kurt.

Brad cleared his throat and prepared to tell a story about being stuck in the research phase. No need for him to know about the target being dead already.

He accepted the call.

Kurt's tone was impossible to read. "Any updates on your assignment?"

He cracked his knuckles. "I'm getting close. That lead on the dark web—"

"He's dead."

"Who?" Brad was so convincing, he almost believed himself.

"Your target!"

"He's dead?"

"That's what I just told you!"

"How'd that happen?"

"That's what I'd like to know," Kurt bellowed. "You didn't find any of his enemies in your research?"

"I wasn't looking for that."

"Shouldn't you be watching him? You should be on his tail, learning his schedule."

"He's a tricky one, like I said. Want me to keep looking?"

"Yes! May as well take advantage of the time you've spent looking into him."

"Anything else I can do for you?"

"Just figure out who killed him!"

Brad held back a smile. "Why are you so upset over this? Target down. We can move on to the next one."

"It isn't that simple."

"Why not?"

"It just isn't. Find out who did it."

"Okay, but I can't help but feel like it would be wasting time."

"It's not. Once you find the person who did this — that's your next target. I'll talk to you later."

The call ended.

Brad stared at the phone.

Kurt wanted him to take out the person who'd killed his target?

That really didn't make sense.

Except under one circumstance.

His boss hadn't really wanted the man dead. He'd expected to have Brad eliminated when he went in for the kill.

Brad was the actual target. And with two opportunities

already gone awry, he would've made certain the job was done right this time.

His mouth dried.

Kurt really did want him dead. He'd been on Brad's side up until Brad mentioned wanting to find his dad's killer.

That could only mean one thing.

Brad's boss *had* been the one to murder Dad.

The room spun around him.

Knock, knock!

"Brad," Faye called from the other side of the door. "My salon's done. I want to show everybody."

Worst timing ever.

But she sounded so excited, there was no way he could ever say no.

"Hold on." Brad closed his eyes and took measured breaths to get himself in the right headspace.

"Hurry!"

"I will." He listened for her footsteps and stood. Stretched. Tried to push away thoughts of his boss trying to take his life.

There were only two ways out of this profession — death or retirement — but he'd done everything in his power to ensure that his was the latter.

From the looks of things, he would have to take out his boss to do that. And even that would have its own consequences. Ralf would be out for blood. Even in his seventies, the man was still a killer. He also knew the most deadly assassins around, people Brad had never met. People who stayed invisible for a living.

Knock, knock!

"I'm ready." He wasn't, but Brad answered the door with a smile anyway. "You're all finished?"

Faye beamed. "Now all I need is to get some clients in here."

That was all he needed — more people in the house while he was plotting the murder of a trained assassin. He held his grin. "Let's see it."

She took his hand and led him down the stairs, talking excitedly about the newly renovated room.

Brad thought only of revenge. The possibilities were endless, but he had to be careful. Like himself, Kurt had an extra set of eyes — always ready for an unexpected attack.

This would be his most challenging target yet, and would require more time than anything before it. But the payoff would make everything worth it.

Finally taking down his father's murderer. The same man who'd sent people to kill him when out on his own assignments. It would be his best reward yet.

"Are you ready?" Faye's voice brought him back to the present, her smile reminding him of their kids on Christmas morning.

"You bet I am." He tried to match her enthusiasm.

The children and his mother were standing just to the side of the door, where they couldn't see into the dark salon.

"Here it is." Faye let go of his hand and opened the door. She turned on the lights and waved everyone in.

They all oohed and aahed as she gave the tour. It had two chairs in front of mirrors and another at a lower sink for washing hair. One wall was painted a soft purple, with posters of men and women with fashionably coiffed hair.

"What do you think?"

Brad kissed her. "I couldn't be happier for you."

Luna jumped up and down. "It's so pretty!"

"Mom, this is amazing." Hadley looked around. "Everyone's going to love it."

"Yeah, it's great. Looks like it's going to be fun for you." Zeke gave an obviously forced smile, but at least he was trying.

Faye stepped back and looked at everyone. "Who wants to help me break in the salon?"

"What do you mean?" Zeke's gaze darted around.

"She means, who wants the first haircut. It should be you." Hadley tugged on one of his curls.

He stepped back, swatting her away. "No chance. You."

She looked at the ends of her hair before glancing at her mom. "I could use a trim. But nothing more."

"Just a trim?" Faye looked around, her gaze landing on Luna.

Their youngest pulled the hoodie over her head. "Not my hair."

"No?" Faye pursed her lips and turned to Brad. "What about you?"

"Me?" He couldn't say no to her eager eyes. "I could probably do with a cut."

"Great!" She turned to Hadley. "Crank the music, and we'll get this party started."

Brad sat in one of the chairs facing a mirror, but Faye led him toward the sink.

"I just washed it this morning."

"This isn't the barber shop." She poked his shoulder and gestured for him to sit.

Before he knew what was happening, his head was in the sink and warm water was heating his scalp. Faye was talking, but he couldn't make out a word because of the stream coming down dangerously close to his ears. She pulled out the faucet and moved it around his head before massaging shampoo onto his head.

He closed his eyes, relaxing despite all the stress

coursing through his body. A fruity smell enveloped him, but didn't last long before she washed the suds away.

A few moments later, Brad was seated in front of the mirror with a towel wrapped around his hair. Faye draped black cape around him and smiled. She opened a drawer, and instead of pulling out scissors or a comb, she aimed her phone at him.

"Why?"

"Because this is the first haircut in my salon."

He held back a groan and gave his best smile — she deserved as much. After she snapped a few pictures, he grabbed the phone and handed it to Hadley. "Now I get a photo kissing the stylist."

Their daughter held up the device and took pictures of them kissing.

"Ew." Zeke crossed his arms, but he was smiling.

The haircut itself went quickly, and though it was shorter than Brad usually wore it, he liked it.

She brushed him off and removed the cape. "Now another picture. This one goes on the wall."

"What?" he exclaimed.

Faye kissed his cheek. "Unless you'd prefer the before photo."

"Or one of us kissing."

She gave him a playful smirk. "That works, too." Then she snapped the picture.

He couldn't complain — not with Faye as happy as she was. And she'd been even more delighted when she didn't have to go into the other salon every day.

Hadley helped sweep the floor, then they all made their way to the kitchen.

His mom went over to the oven and peeked inside. "Perfect timing."

"Did you hear that?" Zeke looked into the living room.

"What?" Brad asked.

His son's face paled. "The news. They said the police just pulled something out of the harbor."

"Why do *you* look concerned about that?"

"Hadley told me."

Brad's stomach knotted. "About … about … the thing?"

"You mean Nate."

Brad turned to Hadley. "Really?"

"You're the one who wanted us to spend more time together!"

"I'm not going to tell anyone," Zeke insisted. "Let's go find out what they pulled out of the water."

Everyone exchanged a mixture of worried and apprehensive expressions, except his mother and Luna, who only looked confused. Even Brad didn't feel so certain all of a sudden — nothing was impossible. But anyone finding that body was as close to impossible as one could get.

Even so, he held his breath between reassuring his family that everything was fine.

Faye sent Luna to her room to look for something, to keep her from seeing what might turn out to be a body.

It didn't help that Hadley was practically hyperventilating.

He put his hand on her back. "Breathe. It's going to be all right."

Her eyes shone with tears. "I hope you're right."

"I am." He gave her a reassuring nod.

A diaper commercial started playing.

Everyone settled on the couch, talking over each other. Once the news came back on, everyone quieted.

A traffic report dragged on for what felt like a decade.

Finally, they returned to the main news story. The boat. More precisely, what it had pulled up after all this time.

It couldn't have taken that long to pull up a body — even with the weights and plastic.

The two anchors rambled on before the screen finally showed the dark harbor with lights shining around the rescue boat. The camera slowly panned around until it reached the other side of the vessel.

Hanging on a large hook was a small, noncommercial plane. It had gone missing the previous year.

Brad's muscles turned to rubber. He leaned against the couch, barely able to catch his breath.

Hadley high-fived her brother before collapsing into her mom's embrace.

"Am I missing something?" Mom asked, turning toward Brad.

He answered fast. "We were all worried it was the kids' missing friend."

"Oh, I see." She nodded knowingly, still looking stumped.

He raked his hands through his hair. "Looks like we can return to life as normal."

Ding-dong!

Dread washed through him. Who could that be?

Zeke hurried to the door.

A moment later, he returned, his eyes wide. "Two cops are on the porch."

Chapter Twenty-Nine

BRAD STARED AT HIS SON. "Are you sure they're police? Not just more social workers?"

"It's them. The same lady who kept coming around after Duke died."

Hadley made an inhuman sound and raced up the stairs, her footsteps thundering.

Faye rushed over and clung to him. "You don't think …?"

He shook his head. "It isn't possible. This has to be about something else."

"What?"

Ding-dong!

Knock, knock, knock!

His mouth went dry. "We'd better go find out."

Brad stood tall and marched toward the door like he didn't have a care in the world. But his stomach was churning acid, he couldn't get a full breath in.

"Brad?" Faye's eyes were full of concern.

"Let me handle this." He stepped away from her and looked through the peephole.

It was Detective Stewart and some bald uniform he'd never before seen. Probably here to ask more questions about Nate.

Brad took a deep breath and answered the door, his expression stoic at first but then softening. He stepped into the crack between the door and the wall. "Detective, it's a surprise to see you. Great news about the plane, isn't it?"

"Yes, but that isn't why I'm here."

"I don't imagine it is. If you speak with the social worker, we've all answered plenty of her questions."

"Social worker?"

Brad nodded. "The one looking into Nate's disappearance. Found any leads on him leaving to find his birth parents?"

She stepped closer, her brows nearly touching. "I'm not here about that, either. You—"

"What, then? I've been proven innocent in Duke and Allison's deaths."

The other officer pulled out handcuffs.

Brad tilted his head. "What's going on?"

"Bradley Morris, you're under arrest."

"For what?" he demanded.

She turned to the officer. "Cuff him."

Brad stepped back. "You can't do this! I haven't done anything."

Faye pulled the door open. "Why are you arresting him?"

Zeke and Mom both began talking.

"Silence!" Stewart held up her hand, glaring at Brad. "Step onto the porch."

"I didn't do anything!" he repeated.

The detective narrowed her eyes. "A bloody knife with your fingerprints all over it says otherwise. Step outside now."

"What bloody knife?" Brad demanded. "Where was it? Who's dead?"

"Come out here, before we have to make a scene."

Brad glanced out past his yard. Neighbors were already gathering on the street and sidewalk. No wondering, considering the police cruiser had its lights flashing for all to see.

He didn't budge. "What knife?"

Her nostrils flared. "We'll discuss this at the station. Step out now, or am I adding resisting arrest to your charges?"

He clenched his jaw, but stepped outside into the biting cold. His shirt was too thin for this weather.

The officer slapped the freezing cuffs on and secured them so tightly they dug into his flesh.

Faye shoved his jacket over his shoulders. "At least let him have a coat!"

He turned to her, grateful. "There's an envelope at the bottom of my nightstand drawer. Call the attorney listed in there. Tell her exactly what's going on, and make sure she goes to the station."

"Right away! Anything else?"

The officer yanked Brad toward the steps.

"She'll tell you what to do."

"Dad!" Zeke reached for him.

"It'll be fine. This is all a misunderstanding. I'll be home as soon as possible."

The officer shoved Brad down the steps and on the walkway toward the cruiser.

Neighbors whispered and pointed. Others boldly asked who he'd killed.

Brad ignored them, while at the same time taking inventory of who came to gawk during his worst moment.

That was when he saw her.

Jacinta Parks, the social worker, standing off to the side, away from the others. It was dark and she was far away, but there was enough light to see the width of her smirk.

Even if she had nothing to do with this, of course she would want to watch.

But Brad had more important things to worry about.

Kurt had framed him for murder yet again.

And Brad had no doubt that this time, he'd made sure it would stick.

A Quick Favor...

If you enjoyed this book, please take a moment to write a short review on your favorite online bookstore so other readers can enjoy it, too.

Thanks so much!

About the Authors

Stacy Claflin is a USA Today bestselling thriller author who has published more than 75 novels, including Girl in Trouble and The Perfect Death. She has always been curious about the human mind, and in her quest to learn more, she earned a degree in Psychology. Her favorite course was Abnormal Behavior, which has been useful in writing fiction.

Her love for thrillers goes back to her early childhood when she fell in love with Unsolved Mysteries and America's Most Wanted. When Stacy was five, she got mad at a babysitter who wouldn't let her watch the evening news. These days, she spends her free time listening to true crime podcasts or watching documentaries on the subject.

She has been telling stories for as long as she can remember, and as child would often get into trouble for trying to convince friends her wild tales were true. Now she puts her creativity to better use by writing page-turning stories that leave readers begging for more.

Nolon King writes fast-paced psychological thrillers set in the glitzy world of entertainment's power players with a bold, insightful voice. He's not afraid to explore the darker side of human nature through stories featuring families torn apart by secrets and lies.

Nolon loves to write about big questions and moral

quandaries. How far would you go to cover up an honest mistake? Would you destroy your career to protect your family? How much of your soul would you sell to get the life of your dreams? Would you cheat on your husband to keep your children safe? Would you give in to a stalker's demands to save your marriage?

Dead For Good

Dead For Good

Left For Dead

Dead Of Night

Wake The Dead

Dead For Life

Once Upon A Crime

Once Upon A Crime

Twice Upon A Lie

Three Times a Murder

Stand Alone Novels

Lost and Found

A Simple Kill

Blown

Miserable Lies

Secrets We Keep

Close To Home

Heat To Obsession

Tell Me No Lies

Fade To Black

www.ingramcontent.com/pod-product-compliance
Lightning Source LLC
Chambersburg PA
CBHW011916130726
47903CB00016B/3108